Miguel Bonnefoy was born in France in 1986 to a Venezuelan mother and a Chilean father. *Octavio's Journey* is his first novel. It has won several awards and was shortlisted for the Prix des Cinq Continents and the Goncourt First Novel Award.

Emily Boyce is in-house translator and editor at Gallic Books.

Octavio's Journey

Miguel Bonnefoy

Translated from the French by
Emily Boyce

Gallic Books
London

A Gallic Book

First published in France as *Le voyage d'Octavio* by
Éditions Payot & Rivages, 2015
Copyright © Éditions Payot & Rivages, 2015

English translation copyright © Gallic Books, 2017
First published in Great Britain in 2017 by
Gallic Books, 59 Ebury Street,
London, SW1W 0NZ

A CIP record for this book is available from the British Library
ISBN 978-1-910477-31-1

Typeset in Fournier MT by Gallic Books
Printed in the UK by CPI (CR0 4YY)
2 4 6 8 10 9 7 5 3 1

I

At the port of La Guaira on 20 August 1908, a ship from Trinidad dropped anchor off the Venezuelan coast, unaware that it was offloading a plague which would trouble the country for half a century. The first cases showed up along the coast among cochineal merchants and sea-bream vendors. Next it was the turn of beggars and sailors, who gathered outside churches and taverns, praying to keep misfortune and shipwreck at bay. Within a week, a quarantine ward had been set up and a national epidemic declared. During the second week, the authorities announced there was to be a rat hunt, with a silver coin paid for every animal killed. By the third week, the sick were being put in isolation; tests were carried out and buboes the size of eggs removed. It was not long before the first fires were lit in yards and sulphur began to waft from shacks. After a month, with the epidemic closing in on the capital, the first wooden saint was carried out at the head of a great procession.

The faithful thronged the narrow streets in a village on the outskirts of Caracas. To a chorus of psalms and hymns, they helped lift up the silver bier on which an effigy of the Nazarene of St Paul, dressed in gold-embroidered purple robes, was carried towards the infirmaries by mulattos. The statue itself was barely visible beneath the piles of orchids, the crown of thorns on its head and the bells and symbolic objects that hung around it. The villagers leant out to watch as the procession of men and women swelled from street to street, to the sound of tambourines and trumpets, and was then guided into front porches where ladies in their chemises, their brows beaded with sweat, reached towards the statue and muttered words that sounded like laments.

Among the houses on the edge of the mountainside was one belonging to a Creole who had planted a sturdy lemon tree – as old, nearly, as he was himself, its fruits twined with mistletoe – against his hedge. The procession approached. The Creole came out with a bolt-action rifle in his hand and a bunch of cartridges tucked under his arm.

'I'll shoot anyone who tries to get past this hedge,' he shouted from his veranda. 'Starting with that wooden one on your shoulders. We'll soon see if saints are immortal.'

The pallbearers turned on their heel without further ado. But as they made to leave, the crown of thorns got caught on a branch of the tree. The Creole shouldered his rifle and, cursing, fired a single shot which echoed down the mountain. The bullet freed the statue from the branch, shook the leaves of the tree and made hundreds of lemons rain down like green buboes on the heads of the faithful and roll as far as the doorsteps of the shacks below.

It was hailed as a miracle. The yellow pulp was used to treat infections, the zests were dried and ground to sprinkle over fish and the air was purified with the fruit's sharp oils. Lemon and ginger were thrown together into cooking pots and passed from door to door, reaching every nook and cranny and bringing succour that two thousand years of medicine had failed to do. A plague that might have lasted ten years was beaten back within ten months.

This is the story of the Lord's Lemon Tree, more or less as it was narrated by the poet Andrés Eloy Blanco in the books of my country.

So it was that the old Creole's house was razed to the ground and a church with stone walls and a dirty wooden floor was built opposite the lemon tree and named, as was the village itself, San Pablo del Limón. A simple basilica without organ or ornament, it had a panelled ceiling and opened out onto a courtyard planted with pomegranate trees. The font never lacked water and hymns rang out from the nave down to the outskirts of the village. The stained-glass windows told the illiterate of the passion and suffering of the Crucifixion while outside the heat hung so heavy that all doors were kept closed until vespers.

No pope came to consecrate the altar and the apse. No sculptures were brought to furnish the cloister. The effigy of the Nazarene of St Paul was propped up against one of the pillars in the nave and women rose before dawn to put coins in the money box beside it. Pilgrims came from far and wide to worship before the statue. The news spread as far as the abbeys. Monks began to arrive, along with gold-diggers, and even a priest who smelt of almonds and nutmeg and knew no Latin, and busied himself with tending the relic.

When the village witnessed its first murder, the first prison and first cemetery were built using the same stones. The narrow streets were awash with thieves and vagabonds stinking of wood and debasement; but there were also hard-working men who had walked from the town to buy goods more cheaply. Mountain- and caravan-dwellers came, Christians following an archbishop's edict, nomads. They stayed a few days and filled up on hot food, all of them claiming to be merely passing through. They would visit the inns and guesthouses, smile at a friendly innkeeper and end up staying for the rest of their lives. On the edge of a small plot of land they would put up a mill, dig a vegetable patch beside a channel of water and, there beneath a sky so rounded that the sun rolled within it, they willingly surrendered to a climate that knew no seasons.

People took to judging the status of a house by the number of windows it had. Road names were written on planks of wood, indicating the people who lived there. The hospital stood on Calle del Hospital, the convent on Calle de las Hermanas; the venerable doctor Domínguez lived on Calle del Doctor Domínguez, while Calle de los Cornudos was not, as the name suggested, a place where cuckolds grew horns, but where cattle lost theirs at the abattoir.

All was music and commotion, mist and sunshine. The irrigation channels became mires where pigs took long siestas, and even the lashing tropical rains could not wash them clean. The frequent noise of mangoes thudding to the ground and cocks fighting in rings could be heard in the distance. The wind carried the sound of cattle lowing as they kicked up dust with their hooves, and the village squares were used for forums, fairgrounds and *paseos*. Stallholders came together beneath palm shades to set up the first markets. Panting beasts climbed uphill laden with baskets of cloves and green chillies, inks and pearls, their spines bending under the weight of caged parrots. Professional writers charged a fortune to compose love letters, old men counted the months in kernels of maize and stallholders told children stories to keep night at bay. These were simple yet fearful times. The village was threatened only by superstition and folk wisdom, and late in the evening it was not unusual to see a man with a rifle slung over his shoulder doing a night round of the square on the back of an ageing donkey.

With time, the bushy, abundant hillside swelled with shacks and groups of buildings in a never-ending blossoming of life. Year after year it was paved with more stones and drew ever more men escaping poverty in the cities. The new arrivals would head for the top of the hill, find a patch of fallow land far from the others and build a home from corrugated iron. As the neighbourhoods expanded, democratic elections had to be held in order to choose a president and a council. The black market began to rival the established trade, while women slept in the shadow of the plane trees when robbed of their husbands by alcohol or misfortune.

The old legends drove the children from their houses. Many were now involved in smuggling, for fear of being excluded, or because it was even more dangerous to remain on the outside. The nights were wild and restless, marred by the crime that lurked around street corners. Girls fell pregnant young and improvised abortions with spoons sterilised in saucepans. It was a road map of wrath. Alas, the saints did not pass through the Venezuelan slums. They did not sit at this particular table. They played no part in the slow and painful construction of the happiness of the poor, who, looking up towards the light, counted their rosaries in olive pits and strained all their senses in order to hear heaven's answer to their prayers.

One day, the statue of the Nazarene disappeared apparently unnoticed. From then on, the church doors often remained locked. The pews were no longer dusted, the floors no longer washed, the galleries no longer decorated with flowers. The pilgrims' tales and their legacy took another path.

During the rainy season, the lemon tree was felled, its bark now teeming with woodworm as the town was with people. It took several mulattos to carry the tree, processing with it to an isolated patch of wasteland. No one came out to join the procession, nor leant out to watch it pass. Not far from the houses, a fire was lit, a reminder of the plague of yesteryear. The smoke hung in the sky for three days. For the last time, the church bells pealed. So it was that half a century after the arrival of the boat from Trinidad, all that remained was the pungent scent of lemon and a church standing among the cypress trees like a lone and sorry mast on a land without ancestors.

II

Don Octavio was born of this land.

He lived on the hillside in a modest, flimsy, slate-clad house to which he held no deeds. The space, which must once have formed a single room, was divided into a living room and bedroom. A wardrobe stood beside a glassless, curtainless window typical of the tropics, with a camp bed and rush-seat chair nearby. At the back of the living room, candles burnt on a little altar, casting flickers of light on the walls. Apostle figures were carved into broom handles and also etched on glasses which had been filled with rum to guard against misfortune. The scent of wild herbs hung in the air.

Octavio welcomed Dr Alberto Perezzo into his living room. He was quite a good doctor, well groomed, with an almost olive complexion. He was always cheerful and jolly, and had a kindly way about him – yet he still complained about the endless zigzagging steps he had to climb up the hillside, house after house, in order to reach his patients. He wiped the sweat from his face with his sleeve. And to top it all off, he admitted with an embarrassed smile, he had left behind his prescription slips. Octavio looked anxiously up at him.

'There's nothing to write on here, Doctor.'

Alberto Perezzo told him not to worry; he would write the prescription in the margin of a newspaper instead.

'They're used to it at the health centre,' he added. 'In this country, we still write on newspapers after they've been printed.'

Don Octavio buttoned up his shirt, then got up and went into the kitchen.

'Sorry, Doctor, but there's nothing to write on here.'

The doctor looked around and saw only a piece of bread and some tobacco on a table by the window. A lump of charcoal lay on the ground at his feet.

'Here's what we'll do, Octavio. I'll write the names of the medicines on the table. I'll come back tomorrow with my pad.'

The doctor leant over and, slowly drawing each individual letter, wrote out the prescription between the grooves of the wood.

'If I'm not back tomorrow, copy it out yourself and tell the chemist I sent you.'

He brushed off the charcoal dust that had rubbed onto his fingers. Beads of sweat were forming again on his brow. He cursed the steps once more, asked for a glass of water and set off, closing the door behind him.

For a moment, Octavio stood before the table. Barely a patch of it had been left unblemished by the bluish rum stains that covered almost all the wood, like the inside of a barrel. The letters drawn on the table were marks of another kind of strange intoxication. He knew immediately that the doctor would not be back the next day. He would be busy applying onion and salt poultices, delivering a teenage mother's baby in the back of a shack, or extracting a bullet fused with a coin from someone's knee amid hoarse cries.

Octavio put the empty glass down on the window ledge. He picked up a table knife and, with a movement repeated so often it no longer caused him pain, cut into the palm of his hand. He watched the blood darken his fingers like splashes of ink. Then he washed his hands in a basin filled with rainwater and bandaged the wound with rags. He lifted the table onto his shoulders, opened the door and set off towards the chemist's.

The sun was already weakening over San Pablo del Limón and the shadows deepened. Thousands of little brick-built houses stretched away up the hillside in a higgledy-piggledy fashion, one on top of the other, with open-air kitchens, empty terraces and hammocks strung between palm trees. The sun warmed the walls and a shimmering mirage was still visible on the corrugated-iron roofs. In the distance, a bare-chested man stood at his window. Women stood under porches, hurrying to finish their cigarettes. Children were throwing stones at a tree to knock down a mango. It might have been a scene from the beginning of the world.

Don Octavio took a meandering path down the steps, with the table on his back. He stopped from time to time to rest in the shade of a billboard, leaning on his table and stumbling over the words written on it. On the way he passed three men who turned to ask gently but firmly if he would lend them the table for a game of dominoes. He joined them at the table, caught up in the spirit of mute camaraderie, covering the ivory pieces in a film of charcoal dust. Further on, he ran into water carriers and workmen going up and down the front steps of a house. His table came to the rescue of a child who had lost all hope of getting his ball down from a roof. With its wooden legs, he was able to fend off two mangy dogs, foaming with rage, and he covered the last stretch of the journey on the back of a truck carrying papayas, whose drivers spoke in words he did not really understand of a coming revolution.

There was a long queue outside the chemist's. When his turn came, his shoulder was dirty from leaning against the roughcast wall. He put the table down before the chemist. But the charcoal had rubbed off on his back: the names of the medicines were no longer legible; a dusty black moiré pattern was all that was left.

'What was the prescription for?' the chemist asked coldly, taking the measure of him.

Don Octavio muttered his excuses. He claimed not to remember and waved his hands around awkwardly, trying to find a trace of a letter in the black dust. He gave the name of the young doctor, but the chemist replied curtly that Perezzo was out. The queue behind him was getting impatient. The chemist looked away, exasperated.

'Come back with a real prescription.'

Octavio began to panic.

'D'you have something to write with?' he asked suddenly. 'Would you write a note for the doctor and ask him to visit me again? I'm Octavio. He knows who I am.'

But the chemist handed him a pen and a sheet of paper.

'Write it yourself, Señor.'

At the sound of these words, all his years of suffering came flooding back. Octavio felt an old sadness making its nest in his heart once more. And so, slowly repeating a gesture he had been making all his life, he took off his bandage and said tonelessly, 'I've hurt my hand. Can't write. P'rhaps you could help me?'

III

Nobody learns how to say he cannot read or write. It is not learnt, but is kept in a nebulous place deep inside, far from daylight, a religion that requires no confession.

Don Octavio had always kept his secret, gouging it into his fist, feigning injury to spare himself the shame of admission. He exchanged only simple words with his fellow humans, words carved out of use and necessity. He had gone through life counting on his fingers, guessing at words by adding up their letters, reading people through their looks and gestures, excluded from the jealous relationship between sounds and letters. He spoke little, barely at all. He mimicked what he heard, sometimes without understanding what he was saying, missing out syllables, making roughly the right sounds, and often the words on his lips were like precious alms. He took from the world only oxygen, and gave it only silence in return.

On reaching school age, he had been denied an education. That was in the days when chapters on native history in primary-school textbooks still described the conquest of the Americas as a 'discovery'. At eighteen, young Octavio did not vote, and signed every form with a shaky cross, the only letter in his alphabet. A simple soul, he defined himself by his very simplicity. He had the forgetful, or perhaps endearingly inattentive, air of a dreamer. He did not know the pleasures of the texture of a piece of paper or the smell of old books. He had learnt to decipher the bus timetable by monitoring the frequency of services, to tell a brand from the packaging and denominations of money by the colour of banknotes. He calculated the cost of a purchase by reading the level of confidence in the vendor's eyes.

As an adult walking down the street, his sole aim was to blend in as an anonymous, average individual, just one more face among a thousand others, an unimpeachable example of reserve and restraint, modesty and decency. He avoided quarrels and violence at all costs, being ignorant of his rights and incapable of defending them. His thoughts were like telegrams, devoid of prepositions. In company he only kept quiet for the shell-like protection of silence, as others only spoke to feel words trip eagerly off their tongues. He was a stranger to beautiful sentences; discretion was his dwelling place. Numbed, he could not see the disadvantages of his silence any more than a wise man can those of his wisdom.

He did casual shifts in shady places, working as both a messenger and a labourer, or waiting on tables in a disreputable bar one night, slogging in a stinking tannery the next. He worked all the hours he could but was not materialistic or greedy, treating his earnings like water drunk only to quench a thirst. He avoided official posts and steered clear of schools. From the nation that had witnessed his birth, he inherited only its stamina and servitude.

It is not living in misery that causes a person to be miserable, but the inability to describe it. For Octavio, this meant he carried a rage within him that ran right through his history, a legacy of anger. Like him, his father used to cut his hand. He could not think of ink without associating it with the metallic taste of blood. He had his father's face, more like marble, wood or stone than a mask, impenetrable as a dense forest. His features were no different from those of any peasant: harsh and rough, with tanned skin and eyebrows as thick as ivy. A hard and shapeless lump of clay, sealed on every side.

Yet in spite of the marks of weariness and age, he did not cut too shabby a figure. He was noticeably taller and broader than the average man. His body might have been hewn from a tree trunk; his heart could beat for a hundred years. He was shaped like a giant with a thick neck, solid thighs, powerful shoulders and a back that was always slightly arched, as if he were carrying an invisible weight. He was strong enough to bring a young ox to its knees simply by holding on to its horns. He did not seem encumbered by his own bulk, but rather seemed to float within it, his movements graceful and fluid, a curious mixture of feather-light and firm. There was an arrogance to his vitality in that it took up every space, leaving no room for anything else. To see him was to be presented with a picture of a whole land of mangoes and battles.

Like a monster or a genie, Octavio was destined to leave the world without descendants. His robustness and passion for life were inherited from a freedom he could pass on to no one else. He was one of those men who, like trees, must die standing up.

IV

The day the young doctor came back to see Don Octavio, a flag was raised in the middle of the slum to show that illiteracy had been eradicated, like a disease. Centres of adult education were set up in disused school wings. Leaflets were distributed outside shops. Posters were put up. A printer opened his factory to teach people how to fold and sew sheets of paper with cotton thread and corrugated cardboard to make their own notebooks. After six thousand years of existence, in some kitchens, writing was being used for the first time to keep a note of spending and recipes.

'The illiterate are now breaking their silence like plague victims,' Alberto Perezzo observed, looking out of Octavio's window at the flag. 'Everywhere you look, they're eager to show their wounds. Yesterday, a gardener was saying he once killed a whole flowerbed because he hadn't been able to tell the difference between weedkiller and fertiliser.'

Don Octavio had already bandaged his hand. He watched the doctor writing the prescription on his pad. The doctor recounted the stories he had been told on his visits, the notes left on his floor, the thank-you letters written in the clumsy and hesitant hand of a first attempt. He held his pen in midair to avoid making a blot.

'Only a couple of days ago, just a few houses down from here, a woman admitted she'd never been able to read the names of the bus stops. She'd spent thirty years counting the stops by moving dried beans from one pocket to the other. Can you imagine, Octavio? Thirty years counting beans!'

As he handed Octavio the prescription, he noticed the bandaged hand he was holding behind his back.

'What happened there?' he asked.

'Just a scratch,' replied Octavio.

'Do you want me to look at it?'

'No need, Doctor.'

The doctor smiled and did not ask again. The sun was going down. The chemist's was still open. It had rained and the route down through the narrow streets and steps would be slippery; better to skirt the slum and go through the surrounding fields. Octavio walked with the doctor as far as the church, then he took the old dirt track that ran behind the houses.

The earth was black, heavy, greasy. Whole hectares of dense, fertile fallow land were drying in the breeze. In the soil, Octavio read the traces of a bird from its tracks, a mouse from its trail of debris, and a mule from the impression of its hooves. He could follow the path a horse had taken from meadow to stable. Further on, among the pine trees, the ferns had been flattened by couples lying down to make love. Names had been carved into beech bark and the huge, strange-looking canopies of the rain trees cast shadows over the pastures. Swept away by the wind, drawings in the sand were like a return to the first art, the first engraving or knotted rope. A return to a world in which you showed what you meant by pointing, and counted the hours by the movement of the light.

When Octavio arrived at the chemist's, he put the prescription down on the counter. The chemist picked it up and eyed it with suspicion.

'I can't make out the last word,' she said eventually.

Don Octavio apologised for not having brought his glasses; he could not read such tiny handwriting without them. She replied that she could not sell him a medicine without being able to read what it was called.

'I'm not trying to trick you,' Octavio said softly. 'I just want to buy what's on this bit of paper.'

They looked at one another, and each discovered in the other's eyes the same dark passageways, the same hovels, the temperamental stove in the corner, the filthy beds pushed close together, the tussles and curses.

'I can't make out the last word,' she concluded curtly in an effort to deny their common roots.

Don Octavio squirmed. He was about to respond when a woman sitting nearby got to her feet. She took the prescription out of the chemist's hands and, in a clear voice that was made for the theatre, read right down to the doctor's signature. The chemist scowled and disappeared into the back room.

The woman might have been older than him, but her elegance and class made her seem more youthful.

'People can no longer read,' she said. 'The times we're living in!'

Don Octavio said nothing. Where he lived, men were not talkative by nature. Discussions were brief and to the point – characterised, in fact, by a lack of discussion.

'Do you sleep on your front?' she asked abruptly, turning to face him.

Before he had a chance to respond, she carried on.

'You shouldn't. Sleeping on your front puts unnecessary pressure on the vital organs – the stomach, liver and intestines. How are your intestines, by the way?'

'Fine, I think.'

'Señor,' she said with great solemnity, 'sleeping on your front can cause diabetes.'

Then, moving on seamlessly, she began telling him how important it was to drink plenty of water during the day to avoid cramp in the legs, but to stop in the evening in order to avoid accumulating excess fluids. She personally relied on pain-relief gels, incense and an array of eye masks to help her sleep. She avoided reading stories with thrilling plots or heated dialogue before bed. Instead, she sought out descriptions of the countryside, and always aimed to drift off on a metaphor.

Octavio watched this woman who was opening her heart to the cold clarity of his own. He studied her fine nose and thin lips. There was as much spirit as there was solitude about her.

He timidly asked her name.

She replied in a powerful voice, as if addressing an entire people.

'*Yo me llamo Venezuela.*'

V

Venezuela suffered from acute insomnia, which meant that for the past twenty years she had had to nap at odd times of the day. She had grown used to irregular bedtimes, sometimes eating in bed and getting up in the middle of the night to roam her apartment. The doctor advised her to stop taking her sleeping pills. Out of embarrassment, she began avoiding pharmacies where she might be recognised and ventured out to the little chemists' shops in the suburbs where she could buy what she needed unnoticed amid the anonymity of the crowd.

Octavio offered to buy the pills for her, to save her the trip out to the barrio. They agreed to meet at Bellas Artes, near the Teatro Teresa-Carreño on Plaza de los Museos, in a little café tucked away beneath an arbour. He waited for her for half an hour, clutching the chemist's bag and watching students kissing among the bamboos in Parque Los Caobos. It was a clear day without a trace of cloud.

As soon as she appeared, red-faced from having scurried along to meet him, he forgot she had kept him waiting. They both smiled at the thought of a coffee. They chose a table in the shade, far from the other customers. She was wearing a pale flowery scarf and earrings shaped like cocoa beans. She kept some amber beads tucked inside a silk pouch around her neck, claiming they had antibacterial properties. She gave off a vegetal aroma, as if she had emerged from loose, damp earth. Don Octavio smelt of talc and bath soap. He carried the scent of a half-century of silence.

A notice on a slate read: 'No coffee or lemonade today.'

Octavio called the waiter over and asked for two coffees. The waiter said nothing but pointed wearily at the sign.

'In that case,' he said, 'we'll have two lemonades.'

The waiter raised his eyebrows. Octavio recognised the look: in the eyes of men, all illiterate people are alike. Venezuela stepped in.

'Our eyesight's not what it used to be, *hijo*,' she said to the waiter.

She turned to Octavio.

'I know a place where nobody writes on slates.'

Then, scowling at everyone in sight, she stood up and took him by the arm.

'They serve coffee in the square.'

They walked together up Avenida México, passing the record market near Brion Bridge. On the other side of Avenida Bolívar, construction had begun on the towers in Parque Central. The dust from the building site made Venezuela sneeze. She began talking about the link between inhaling carbon dioxide and developing lung disease, and was still talking at Plaza La Candelaria.

They sat against the wall of the basilica. On the other side of the square, six old ladies in flowery blue dresses were sitting on plastic stools, waving fringed fans and looking over at Octavio and Venezuela. The hairstyles the old maids wore had once been fashionable. They still observed the customs of an earlier time, speaking in proverbs and singing widows' waltzes, and had the strange habit of adjusting their hair before picking up the phone. In these white tropical baroque surroundings, they sold figurines of saints and apostles, along with plastic reliquary statues on little reredos.

Venezuela appeared to have mixed feelings about religion. She railed against the commercialisation of faith and the wealth of the

Church, and then bought – at a vastly inflated price – two votive candles to light in memory of deceased loved ones.

'You never know,' she sighed.

From that point on, she didn't stop talking.

She liked her job, hated spending money, and had many whims. She was a woman of healthy, sometimes bold opinions, yet believed in fated encounters. Several times she stopped abruptly in the middle of the road to tell the story of a particular building, half of which she knew, the rest she made up.

She explained that her father had named her Venezuela in a burst of patriotism. The area she had grown up in was bordered by oil fields, strung together like a beaded necklace. There in Maracaibo in western Venezuela, it was so hot you could fry eggs on car bonnets. In the town squares, men in ties dozed beneath the mangroves while the women stood, flagging, breathless, seeking shade beneath telegraph poles. At certain times of day, the air was so heavy that flies, lacking the energy to fly away, submitted to swatting instead. Everything – shops, schools, bazaars, lottery stalls – closed a little before midday and did not reopen until around four when the shadows began to lengthen.

'That's how Maracaibo came to be known as the coldest city in the world,' she explained. 'There wasn't a single place that wasn't cooled by fans, air-conditioning or cooling units. That's why on the day the dictatorship fell, on 23 January 1958, and the country was liberated with weapons that were hot from the afternoon sun, everyone waited until the evening to join the revolution.'

She was told she had the makings of a good actress and went to live in Caracas. She played parts in vaudeville farces, performed in Greek tragedies, and even appeared at the Teatro Nacional singing *zarzuelas*. To prove it, she asked Octavio to choose one at random. He was flummoxed. All he knew of theatre was the word itself.

Eventually, she felt the need to make her situation clear.

'I've never married. When you spend your life being listened to, you end up judging men by their silence. And since no man can keep his mouth shut for long …'

And so she had gone through life as one crosses a desert: alone, but with great poise, dignity and the composure of a woman used to playing out her existence under the gaze of men.

Octavio listened, staring into space, feeling his heart swell. Every now and then he would ask a brief question before withdrawing into himself again. Everything sounded different in this woman's voice, had a resonance he had never encountered before. She would answer him playfully, revelling in the madness of walking arm in arm through the centre of town with an illiterate stranger. It was a means of defying – but not denying – the world. And although well past the age of burning desires, each of them sensed a flicker of those early emotions being rekindled in the other. Together they let themselves be drowned in the intoxication of the moment, one filling her imagination, the other dismantling the void inside him.

Octavio let himself be led to Plaza Bolívar, which was full of children and black squirrels. Venezuela said the café she had in mind was close by, but when they arrived outside, the shutters were down. Taking the matter in hand, she exclaimed, 'Why don't we have coffee at my place?'

Octavio made an enigmatic gesture suggesting both gratitude and refusal. Not knowing how to respond, he mumbled his agreement.

*

Venezuela's apartment consisted of one large, lofty room with light pouring through floor-to-ceiling windows onto coloured tiles. There were mahogany armchairs and tapestry wing-back chairs and landscape paintings on the walls. A breeze slipped in through an open window, heavy with noises and smells.

She handed Octavio a coffee sweetened with honey. Given the time of day, she opted for tea instead.

'Coffee rattles the nerves, and restless nights can cause strokes.'

She had stuck a sheet of paper on the side of a pillar on which she noted down, night after night, the time at which she had begun to feel sleepy, how she had felt upon waking, and the effects of caffeine.

'See how much I've improved. After a bad night, I make myself a plantain tea in the morning, always checking the leaves haven't turned brown. After lunch, I'll have agave syrup and, if it's very hot, half a glass of lemonade. Sometimes, before it gets late, I rinse my eyes with a little rose water or dragon-tree sap and, if I'm in a lot of pain, I rub my temples with grapeseed oil.'

Octavio had stopped listening. His eye had been drawn to a picture, or rather a stone, a long tablet with strange markings which looked like reptiles, crocodiles or other animals, along with a series of perfectly drawn circles, some floating alone, others joined in a neat spiral.

'What's this?' he asked.

'They're indigenous hieroglyphics,' replied Venezuela. 'You see them in the forests of San Esteban, on the Campanero stone.'

Don Octavio spent a long time looking at these landscapes of chalk and rock, where nothing resembled man, but nonetheless belonged to him.

'Some say they were discovered by the German painter Antonio Goering,' Venezuela went on, 'others that it was Lope de Aguirre's soldiers, or Villegas, before he founded Borburata.'

'What do they mean?'

'I don't know. There are some amazing interpretations in Aristide Rojas's books. They may be to do with tribal feuds among the communities of Lake Valencia, between the Tacariguas and the Araguas. Or they could simply be a way of expressing the natural world.'

Octavio traced the lines with his finger, trying to decipher them. He saw in the jumbled marks of the stone the human tissue of the barrio where he lived, a world freshly born out of nothingness. The flavour of language began with guava, maize and araguaney.

Venezuela poured him a little more coffee and picked up the saucer of honey.

'It only takes a few strokes to write what you mean,' she said. 'For example …'

She dipped her lips in the honey before pressing them against a sheet of blank paper. The trace of two amber-coloured arcs was left behind.

'See … that's how you write the word "kiss".'

She pointed to a tree by the entrance of the building.

'Look,' she said, no longer using the polite form of address.

On one of its branches, where the wood was bent like an elbow, Octavio saw two birds singing as they built their nest in the nook.

She whispered, 'And that's how you conjugate the verb "to love".'

Without knowing exactly what love was, Octavio turned to her, took her face in his hands and kissed her. All the words on her lips were suddenly reduced to this kiss, this tremor, becoming as mute as flesh. Octavio kept his mouth pressed to hers for a long while, as if to leave his mark.

Venezuela pulled back and shook her head. She was afraid

of going too far. The same gulf had always stood between her and men. This was not about Octavio's kiss. It was a distance prescribed by nature. But he kissed her again, and his passion surprised her. She felt a sudden urge to be marooned with him. They were unlike one another in every respect. And yet perhaps, without knowing it, she was deciphering an unknown alphabet beside him, a primordial promise, like the first writing on stone, where everything seems to begin.

VI

Closed since the plague years, the church of San Pablo del Limón had long stood derelict. Bricks had been thrown through the stained-glass windows and there was graffiti on the walls. All that was left of the tilework was a few loose stones overgrown with brambles. Time had warped the building's frame and the paving around the entrance had been lifted by tree roots.

But inside the church, the space was clean, bright and tastefully furnished. The prayer kneelers were covered in packets of imported cigarettes, foreign-made soap, hundreds of bottles of oil and tubs of powdered milk, as well as a stockpile of contraband whisky. Lengths of Genoese velvet and bundles of gold leaf were heaped up on the daises. Along the aisles, utopian landscapes were depicted on blue brocade like old Gobelin tapestries. There were armchairs and cabinets covered in silky fabrics and encrusted with onyx, untouched by the passage of time. Ambassadors' swords, soutanes and long cassocks with damask buttons were stacked on camphor-wood shelves. A society woman's barely worn jewellery sparkled in a jumbled heap at the bottom of a chest of drawers, jostling for space with china wise men and doves. It was like a vanished country in which wealth, in moderation and in excess, was cloaked in simplicity.

The apse was curtained off behind a semicircle of purple drapes, through which shafts of light shone in. There, a group of men and women sat at a table around a tabernacle filled not with the Host, but hundreds of keys on strings.

A man standing by the table in an elegant ivory liqui-liqui

suit buttoned up to the neck began to touch the keys one by one, jangling them between his fingers. Each one had been labelled with an address and put onto a ring. The man in the liqui-liqui looked concerned.

'Anything from the Mole?' he asked all of a sudden.

'The lady of the house is in Valencia on Wednesday and Thursday,' a woman replied. 'The husband is heading out of town on Tuesday.'

'Until when?'

'Still waiting for his lover to confirm. Back in time for the weekend, probably.'

'And the architect?'

'Not this week,' said a man further away. 'The architect hasn't bought anything in a month.'

'No news on the hotel?'

'The Chinese man is moving rooms every two days,' another woman explained. 'He's so jittery he must be scared to look in the mirror.'

'How much are we talking?'

'More than we thought.'

'Let's not lose our Chinese friend, please. This calls for tact, discretion, qualities without which we'd still be swiping watches in supermarkets and selling stolen tyres. We need to look the part … we're not rich enough to be badly dressed.'

He took a gilded silver key from the bunch, closed the tabernacle and turned to face the group like a true man of the world.

'Tonight the cabinet-maker is going to an important event in Los Teques. It's far enough away for us to take our time. Let me say it again: these are works of art we're dealing with. They must be handled with care and delicacy. It's for you to choose between prison and your morals. Make your own minds up … I've made my choice – and here I am. So, if you please, a little savoir-faire.'

Rutilio Alberto Guerra, known as Guerra, uttered this last phrase with an unexpected French flourish. On his orders, two women were put on the Chinese case and the Mole was assigned to the architect's apartment.

He stood tall. At first glance, he looked more like an artist than a bandit. He was a thoughtful burglar with a polite approach to theft and an unparalleled sense of remorse and drama. A bankrupt, a counterfeiter and a clown, he had been a pharmacist, a taxidermist, a welder and a furrier. He had made a name for himself as a young man by picking up dusty paintings, dubious books and worthless clocks from junk shops, inventing fascinating back stories for his acquisitions and then selling them on at vast profit.

'I am, after all, a simple man of the people,' he explained.

Everyone knew he came from a distant place, his homeland an unending succession of hastily left towns. He was a gifted orator, who chose his words carefully to fit the occasion, and never planned a crime without the use of rhetoric.

He slept on the altar, his head resting on the tabernacle of keys, with rugs hanging overhead. He liked to place a taffeta beauty spot beside his nose like a French marquis and walk around with his hands behind his back, surveying all his stolen marvels. He was often accompanied by a stunning mulatta famed for her beauty, who browsed the rooms of the church with fountain pen in hand, making an inventory of the bric-a-brac. It was all meticulously arranged, categorised and then slowly disposed of bit by bit in order to avoid attracting attention. Some items were eventually sold back to the very people from whom they had been stolen.

When he walked, a sense of great destiny seemed to follow in his wake. He appeared convinced his simple presence in history was sufficient to give writers of history books the inspiration for their finest pages. After a short time in the desert, he had come to the conclusion that humanity could only rebuild itself in enclosed spaces, safely holed up on islands or swarming together in colonies like ants. That was how he had come to choose the barrio of San Pablo del Limón, and specifically the old church, as the base for his band of men and women to build their vision of utopia.

Here, banditry was spoken of with respect, like an art or a highly skilled profession. Guerra had surrounded himself with a brotherhood of seasoned burglars who resembled alchemists, all of them nostalgic for the days of decorum and fair play. The proceeds of the booty were collected in a kitty and shared out equally. Most of the thieves followed the Gospel, others improvised prayers to the Virgin Mary, the saints and the occupants of the cemetery. There were no poet-villain Lacenaires, Villons or Caravaggios among them. These were simply men who had come from nowhere, carrying out a cruel job with passion and dedication.

The burglaries they committed were carefully targeted. Nothing was left to chance: they knew where to break in and how to escape. Guerra insisted on the proper upkeep of their vehicles and would not tolerate poor timekeeping. Yesterday the church had welcomed parishioners, rung its bells for Mass and held services. Today it was occupied by humans surviving alone amid the myrtles without Mass or offices, who had relieved men of their fortunes and God of His house.

Don Octavio's role in the brotherhood was to do the cleaning. He moved furniture, washed floors, redecorated the church interiors and restored cornicing, thus repaying the favours that wealth takes from servitude.

He played no part in the burglaries. He stayed behind in the barrio while the rest made for bourgeois houses built for winter, fitted with chimneys that were never lit. As a result he spent most of his time alone in rooms lined with books stolen from libraries or collectors, row upon row as far as the eye could see. He waited hours for the car to return, sitting on a ruby-studded chair that had been wrapped up ready to be sold on, surrounded by biographies of famous men – though famed for what, he didn't know. It was he who had asked not to take part in the burglaries. He preferred to wait, preferred this prison. When he heard the tyres crunching on the gravel outside the church, he would go and help bring in the booty without asking questions. The task was carved out on the wood inside him. He had a broad back, mottled knees, a spine like a flagpole. Despite the heavy burden of loneliness he did not bend beneath the weight of his duty: he carried it uncomplainingly, and so released the others from it.

Guerra had planned the cabinet-maker's burglary with chivalrous concern, like a highwayman in trimmed shirt-cuffs. He sought to pepper his speech with ethics.

'You see, this taste for punctuality and thoroughness, for things to be neatly folded and unfolded, is precisely what led me into this extraordinary profession. Do you see me carrying weapons? Can you imagine me committing a murder? Let's leave that to the also-rans, the small-timers. The way I go about burgling a house is like a writer sitting down to compose a poem. It is meticulously arranged in a breath of inspiration, treading a fine line between a necessary wrong and a necessary word.'

He never wore any colour except white, to ensure he shone in any light. A meditative silence descended as he approached the centre of the altar, deep in thought.

'I'll take El Negro and Carita Feliz with me,' he said. 'Octavio will wait for us here – we'll have heavy items to unload when we return.'

'What items?' asked El Negro.

'We're burgling a cabinet-maker. He has a house full of wooden furniture.'

'Why steal wood when you can steal diamonds?'

'Anyone know a place where you can steal diamonds?' Guerra asked no one in particular. 'May I remind you that Christ was crucified on a wooden cross? That the Library of Alexandria was built of wood? Your mother lay on a plank of wood to give birth to you. Show a little respect.'

At that point, the lone voice of El Negro piped up again, a weedy, bitter little voice.

'May as well burgle a forest,' he said. 'I suggest we put it to a universal vote.'

'What for?'

'We hold a vote and see if the majority agrees with your idea, or not.'

'It's not *my* idea. It's *our* burglary.'

'Let's leave that to democracy to judge.'

Guerra, more than anyone, represented the vanity of the old republics. He came from a time when people were forbidden from meddling in affairs of State, and had held on to the principles of that earlier age.

'Democracies aren't always right,' he reminded El Negro.

El Negro jeered.

'What's so funny?'

'If you don't allow democracy to work, then you'll always be wrong.'

Guerra took this as an attack not only on his politics but his place at the heart of the group. Since most of the burglars did nothing but stare back wordlessly, he announced they would vote with a show of hands.

A murmur went round the table as though hustings were taking place, and El Negro raised his voice in objection. He said it was written in the constitution that any vote must be carried out by secret ballot. Finding himself faced with little choice in the matter, Guerra glanced at his watch and asked Octavio to improvise a ballot box from an ossuary.

They proceeded to vote around the altar in silence. For the first time, Don Octavio exercised his electoral right. A little deliberative assembly gathered after the count. El Negro looked up and said in the most neutral of voices, 'Someone cast a blank vote.'

All eyes turned to Octavio, whose hands were stuffed inside his pockets to hide the scar on his palm.

'That was me,' said Guerra. 'Kings don't vote.'

Then, like a priest speaking from the pulpit, El Negro took the voting slips in his hand and declared beneath the arches of the nave, 'The motion is passed. Now we have a legitimate mandate to steal.'

VII

There was nobody at the cabinet-maker's house, yet every room was inhabited.

On the decorative screens that lined the walls, lions were pulling chariots, stags fighting off packs of wolves and soldiers blowing trumpets. There were carvings on every beam and masks hanging from every joist. Butterflies with dusty wings fluttered under glass cloches and in the hallway stood a wooden sarcophagus engraved with reapers sidling up to dairy maids. The shelves held maps of savannahs and portrait miniatures, and all of Genesis was depicted on a rustic rug. The empty house seemed to have a population of thousands.

Guerra climbed a floating staircase to the mezzanine. On the first floor was a collection of antique books and several walnut dressing tables. Through the shadows he made out the shape of an elegant corniced wardrobe which almost filled an arched recess in the wall. Its doors were fastened with a crémone bolt, and a picture of a giant crossing a river was carved into the veneer.

They began searching for the key, looking for false bottoms in the furniture, taking up rugs, peering behind verdure tapestries, but in vain. They considered taking off the door panels, but they were screwed in too tightly. Someone suggested forcing the lock, but Guerra forbade anyone to touch it.

'You can see it's original!' he chided.

He sat down on the bed, removed his balaclava and held his head in his hands. Powerless before the locked cupboard, he decided on a different course of action. He picked up the telephone and, in a flash of inspiration, dialled a number.

Fifty kilometres away in the town of Los Teques, the cabinet-maker was doing up his flies in the toilets at a society ball when he was called to reception. He was surprised to find the phone call was from his own number.

'Good evening, Señor,' said Guerra in his most professional voice. 'I'm at your house, sitting on your bed admiring the marquetry wardrobe that adorns your bedroom. I consider myself something of an amateur collector and I immediately recognised your eye for geometric design. Allow me to congratulate you on possessing such a piece, Señor. I'm very familiar with your work; I've read most of your articles. You cannot imagine how highly I respect your efforts to preserve an almost forgotten craft. I spent my childhood making marquetry out of wallpaper, scraping the glue off, cutting bits out. Of course, it was only cheap furniture … not up to your standards. Nevertheless, it gave me a taste for decoration. And I always knew there were men like you who were quietly working away at keeping this sadly neglected art alive. It's an honour for me to find myself in your home, Señor. Let me tell you: you're a poet.'

Flustered, the cabinet-maker threatened to call the police. But he was so deeply moved by Guerra's words, he decided against it. It was as if his work had never before been truly seen; as if, after years of secret toil, the result of his labours had finally been unveiled to himself and others, and the cabinet-maker heard himself whisper with great sincerity, 'Much obliged, Señor.'

With no hesitation, Guerra went on.

'I'll steal only a few more minutes of your time. Could you possibly enlighten me as to the variety of wood you've used. Is it purple heart or rosewood?'

'Purple heart.'

'I believe I spot some Boulle-style tortoiseshell on there too. Now tell me, are those parts inlaid in the veneer?'

'No. They're stuck on with an animal glue.'

'You have no idea of the extent to which our lines of work overlap. I have a fear of coming unstuck myself.'

The cabinet-maker fell silent. He found himself facing a large mirror. He was pale.

Guerra continued.

'The reason for my call is to ask you to kindly tell me where I might locate the key.'

'The wardrobe belongs to me,' replied the cabinet-maker, choking back tears.

'But I have the upper hand.'

'Have you forced the lock?'

'Not yet. I've only got an axe with me. How much force do you think the wood can withstand?'

The cabinet-maker began to worry.

'Just as I thought,' Guerra went on. 'That's settled, then. If you're going to keep the key from me, I'll keep my light touch from you.'

'Take my bookcase, then,' the cabinet-maker offered in an attempt to bargain with him.

'I thought you were an intelligent man.'

'Take my amphoras. They're worth a fortune.'

'Your amphoras are so old I'd rather steal the dust they're covered in.'

All at once it seemed to Guerra as if the whole country was listening, and he added, 'Señor, the people will take back their dignity with an axe, since it was with an axe that it was taken from them.'

'I'm calling the police.'

'Let's keep this courteous, shall we?'

'The truth ...' the cabinet-maker admitted. 'The truth is that I've got the key with me.'

This confession allowed Guerra one of the finest moments of his career, a moment destined to live long in the memory. This was no longer a matter of one man's pig-headedness, but that of a whole race of burglars who refused to give in to the lies of oligarchs. He chose his words carefully as if standing before a court and, with that tendency to excess that could lead either to calamity or greatness, calmly explained, 'Señor cabinet-maker, an amateur burglar would believe you. A shrewd burglar would not. And a burglar like me would invite you to fuck off. I'm generous enough to call and keep you informed on the progress of your burglary, and this is how you choose to repay me.'

'I didn't mean to offend you.'

'Oh, you didn't offend me.'

'I mean it, Señor.'

'As do I. This has gone on long enough.'

'I'm begging you.'

'It's time to unbury the hatchet.'

The cabinet-maker was so rattled he ended up telling Guerra where the key was hidden, on condition that he take good care of the wardrobe. Guerra had the good grace not to thank him. After exchanging a few niceties, they ended the call with the usual polite formulas.

'You see,' Guerra told the others, unable to conceal his pride. 'Stealing isn't enough. It takes talent, too.'

Inside the wardrobe they found a five-stringed guitar, two hourglasses and a large object shrouded in a white sheet. Guerra's hand shook as he lifted the cloth.

He pulled it gently away and before his eyes there stood, shining and immortal, drenched in history, the statue of the Nazarene of St Paul with its gold-embroidered purple robe, crown of thorns and scent of bygone processions, its face torn open by the bullet the old Creole had shot at it fifty years earlier.

VIII

'Follow the grassy tracks up the hill, keep to the right when you come to the petrol pump and bear left as soon as you see a broken traffic light. Go past the baseball pitch, keeping the little mango forest on your right. Take the very first diagonal turning onto a road with no name. It's not the first building, or the second, but the one at the end, hidden behind the four tallest palm trees on the road.'

Don Octavio followed these instructions with mathematical precision. Venezuela came to greet him on the doorstep, smiling out of the corner of her mouth and flirtatiously bringing her hand to her chest as if to hide herself from view.

During his time at her home, his writing improved. It no longer faltered, but was clear and regular. He happily rewrote any passage containing mistakes. From time to time his ungainly fingers crushed the lead of the pencil and Venezuela would laugh at his clumsiness. Using a table knife, he would roughly cut the pencil back into shape, bending over it as if sharpening a spear on a grindstone. She never interrupted him. She treated his excesses like a creature to be nourished.

For several days Octavio was confused by the *u* in *gu* and perplexed by the tilde on *ñ*, never having noticed the accent before. She made him hiss to make an *s* and pinch his nostrils for *n*. She taught him to link his thoughts, to swap words around or join them together. He took sentences apart, weighed every syllable. He confused definite and indefinite articles, saw no difference between synonyms, and never managed to make the verb agree with its subject.

One morning, he was surprised to discover how simply the word *mujer* was spelt.

'I expected a more difficult word for such an important person,' he exclaimed.

For a long time afterwards he continued to roll the syllables of the word in his memory, moulding it to his own shape, his mind at once full and aware of all it was lacking.

When he managed to read a whole sentence straight through and was struck with the sudden realisation he had understood it, he felt a pressing urge to rename the world from its very beginnings. He felt somehow bound to a new land, part of the same fight, the same era. Happiness spun around him, and he spun with it. Each word resonated in his mouth like a promise.

His preference was for the lighter-sounding adjectives. He recognised in them the simplicity and tragedy of his own nature. He understood that grammar had traditions beyond its rules. And if he did not share every doubt with Venezuela, it was in order to avoid unnecessary complication, and not because he was afraid to do so.

He stopped cutting into his palm. He no longer filled the basin before he went out or prepared strips of cloth to tie round his hand. The gap had now been filled by the orchestra he heard every evening, an intoxicating whirl of music which he recreated at home later with the sobriety of a single instrument. For, as with women, all Octavio had known of words till then was their dying wave, the expectation that they would vanish as soon as they emerged from his mouth, like the line a sword draws through water. But now he was discovering he could hold on to the trace they left behind, blending the names of things and the things of love. In a single stroke, he could etch both his desire and the mark of that desire. Thirsty for learning as one thirsts for love, he never tired of mixing the two alphabets. There was something illegible in the time they spent together.

For several months, Octavio's work within the brotherhood and his afternoons with Venezuela brought him a sense of fulfilment he had rarely known before.

Business was going so well at the church that it was sometimes hard to find space for new arrivals. If a medieval suit of armour was brought in and needed to be sold straight on, Don Octavio would make it gleam by frantically buffing the cuirass and brigandines, the hauberk and the rondels, the whole body from the helmet to the greaves. He would find himself making the same rubbing movements later under Venezuela's stern gaze, when he got a syllable wrong and had to use the other end of the pencil to erase his crossings-out. If a table with legs representing fantastical creatures was received, he had to clean the glass with vinegar and lemon and remove traces of limescale with coarse salt; those creatures would reappear later in another beautiful setting, on the old illuminated maritime maps that Venezuela showed him and explained at length. Though inside the church he cleaned and polished, it was at Venezuela's house that, without cloth or feather duster, by way of words alone, he made clear what had been murky, made newly appealing what had once been dull. Everything he achieved through his daily toil seemed to be elevated and sweetened in her company.

One night at the church, while tidying a bookshelf, he sat down in a faux-leather armchair that had been turned towards the wall, and opened one of the books on his lap. He turned to a page where an allegory of Literature, depicted as a tall woman in silk robes, stood pale and silent with a lyre in her hand before a stony-faced assembly.

He thought of Venezuela. It seemed impossible to him that Literature should look so unlike a real woman. Literature should hold its pen like a sword and stand amid the vast, uproarious community of men, staunchly defending the right to put names to objects, for she was shaped from the same clay and muck, the same absurdity, as those who served her. She should have loose hair, torn clothing and a heroic air, wear a machete in her belt or a shotgun over her shoulder. Literature should also represent those who did not read her, she should exist in the same way as air and water, and evolve constantly. As his mind wandered, he was overwhelmed by sleep and dozed off in the stony chill, alone and forgotten, with stuffed lambs gathered about him as if he were an angel.

'Donkeys, gentlemen!' cried Guerra. 'Yes, long may the donkey be the protector of our art!'

Octavio woke with a start. He shuffled, hunched, towards the small group assembled around the altar.

'To the donkey who has pulled the carts of great men, dragging their petty obsessions from place to place, who over the centuries has served as messenger, artisan, envoy, confidant and counsellor, who has moved whole libraries, who has shown that the mute servant is the one with most to tell. I once knew a man who hid three hundred gold coins in a donkey's belly. Yes, long may the donkey be the protector of our art!'

Judging this to be sufficient by way of preamble, Guerra opened the tabernacle. He took out a key and passed it round the group.

'This key opens the door to an apartment whose owners will

soon receive an invitation to hear Berlioz's *Requiem* at Teatro Teresa-Carreño. The *Requiem* is three hours long. I don't wish to take any risks. We'll stay in the apartment for an hour. We're looking for a stone.'

'A stone?' El Negro objected.

Guerra slowly turned to face him.

'This is not just any stone,' he replied. 'It's a matter of politics.'

'You can't squeeze money out of a stone.'

'Are you suggesting we take another vote?'

'Not over something as crazy as this. I've got better things to do.'

Guerra stared long and hard at El Negro, then stepped up onto the altar and made an announcement that startled everyone present.

'If you've got better things to do ... then Octavio can take your place.'

Octavio looked up at Guerra in horror. A shiver ran through him and his heart felt as tight as a fist. Weakly, he tried to protest, stammering his excuses, but a rebellious scrum was forming in the nave which quickly got out of hand. Guerra faced the mob from the altar, waving his arms in panic as the gang of burglars surged towards him. From a distance, the scene strangely foreshadowed the one that would be seen a few days later under the roof of the Teresa-Carreño, as the conductor moved his arms with similar flourish to give his musicians the beat of the *Requiem*.

As the meeting descended into total chaos, Guerra declared the session closed. El Negro stormed out of the church crying tyranny.

'This is no utopia,' he shouted on his way out. 'It's a henhouse!'

Guerra calmly returned the key to the tabernacle. He glared at Octavio.

'You'll drive,' he told him.

Octavio asked for the address.

'It's not far,' replied Guerra, stepping down from the altar. 'You follow the grassy tracks up the hill, keep to the right when you come to the petrol pump and bear left as soon as you see a broken traffic light. Go past the baseball pitch, keeping the little mango forest on your right. Take the very first diagonal turning onto a road with no name. It's not the first building, or the second, but the one at the end, hidden behind the four tallest palm trees on the road.'

IX

A few days later Venezuela duly received two invitations for Berlioz's *Requiem*. Without hesitation she asked Don Octavio to join her. He refused, offering no explanation.

Teatro Teresa-Carreño had put on a huge production: thirty-eight brass instruments and hundreds of strings, four orchestras with almost three hundred singers and a Russian tenor soloist who, a few days before his departure, gave a bayan performance to the schools of San Agustín. The 2,300 seats of the theatre were filled for a week. The orchestra pit below the stage was littered with scores and music stands. It was dense with melody.

Whilst programmes were being handed out at the entrance of the theatre, outside the church, Guerra was distributing black canvas balaclavas that covered everything but the eyes. He got into the car singing the *Dies Irae* and, noticing the empty space where El Negro would have sat, remembered their falling out.

'Better to lose a limb than to lose your soul,' he sighed. 'If it was the other way round, we'd all have turned to banditry, repeat offending or, worse, revolution.'

He threw one last glance at the church.

'And to think all this began with a stolen apple.'

When they arrived at Venezuela's apartment, the sky was red.

Octavio was the one who opened the door. He recognised the squeaky hinges and uneven floor tiles. The wall of coloured glass windows, the tapestries, the mahogany furniture: everything was in its place. The scent of honey and beeswax, the table he had bent over to write on, the tree out on the balcony were all familiar to him.

To Guerra's surprise, Octavio did not feel his way along the walls but strode across the room to the pillar where the rock carving hung. But as he went to touch it, he heard a floorboard creak in the next room. Then nothing. Just a sense of something caught in the shadows like a prisoner. He lifted the stone and made for the front door. He was tiptoeing out when he heard another creak and a voice behind him suddenly said,

'Put that down or I'll shoot.'

Guerra just managed to hide behind the door. Don Octavio spun on his heels. Venezuela was standing a few metres behind him holding a beaten-up old gun, wearing an iridescent dress, perfumed and made-up as if about to go out. Finding herself overwhelmed with tiredness as she so often was, she had decided to lie down for a few minutes before leaving for the concert. She had been asleep for an hour.

Don Octavio put the stone down. The balaclava kept his face hidden. He stood up to his full height and the sheer size of him made Venezuela quake. She adjusted her aim.

'You can't squeeze money out of a stone. What do you want, Señor?'

Don Octavio said nothing. Before now, he had only known her to speak softly and sensitively, uttering words of affection. Now the look in her eyes alarmed him. She was afraid.

'What you are doing, Señor, is undermining a country's foundations,' she said, her throat tight with both fear and anger. 'Steal this stone and you steal them all. Then how do you expect roads to be built?'

He said nothing for some time, sensing himself discovered. He knew he would never be able to come back to Venezuela's home.

But he also knew he could never return to the church. Guerra had already left. And there, stripped of all identity, doubly abandoned, Octavio understood that he was signing a pact with exile. Slowly repeating a gesture he had been making all his life, he raised his hand and murmured, 'That's how you conjugate the verb *to steal*.'

The look of horror on Venezuela's face was as intense as the look of shame on Octavio's. Her legs wobbled. She gently put the gun down, keeping her eyes on him.

'Octavio?' she asked, her voice catching in her throat.

The air encircled them, trapping them as if between the pages of a book. Octavio did not remove his balaclava. They stared at each other, not seeing. Slowly, with no haste or drama, he turned away and left Venezuela behind him, perhaps for the last time. A void had opened up like a landscape before them, between them, a chasm that was already closing over.

Across town, the final notes of a requiem had just been played.

X

D on Octavio left the barrio in the middle of the night. He took the road west in a truck with rosaries hanging from the rear-view mirror and got off at a building site near Maracay.

For a few bolivars, he carried sacks of sand, limewashed walls, ground cement, mixed plaster and repointed brickwork. He spent broken nights inside huts, was often hungry and felt he was going mad. The dust irritated his eyes. He worked hard and kept out of trouble, and soon people were asking him to decorate the front of their houses. He would stand on a stepladder to paint window grilles and external beams with weeds growing out of their cracks. All he was given to eat were cold arepas, buttered with his finger.

He took the path between Henri-Pittier National Park and Lake Valencia. His height got him noticed. Offers were made to him – he refused them all, steering clear of petty criminals and smugglers, and preferring to wander alone.

He passed through the villages of Aragua, which had grown up around the mission stations and the first tobacco plantations. Now indigo, sugar cane and cotton were sown there. In thick forest, he lay down on his stomach and drank from the stream. In glades, he stole malanga and yams. One day he saw a ribbon of smoke in the distance – a cabin for road-menders, perhaps, or an old sugar mill, and he heard Joropo tunes being sung. Men were tending the soil, pressing olives and crushing sugar cane in old wooden casks.

Here Octavio spent months working all hours for two Colombian brothers, oiling machinery and sometimes pulling the levers himself. At the end of each day, the brothers would count the piles of crushed sugar cane and calculate his pay at a piece rate. They let him sleep inside a grain store, but sleep wouldn't come.

He took the road towards Valencia and sometimes, for want of work, he was forced to take handouts. The roads were ablaze with colour and voices when the Virgin was carried in a procession around the old coffee fincas. Members of the religious brotherhoods were allowed to ask for alms. They went from door to door with a crucifix and a begging bowl, swapping coins for novenas. Octavio spent two days picking up the money that had fallen from their cassocks and sweeping up the chains and trinkets that lay on the ground. He begged for the cassavas left on altarpieces. He would wait for closing time at eating places, and once, in the backyard of a restaurant, he dined on leftover yucca from customers' plates, as a girl washed tablecloths next to him.

His skin took on a sandy hue, as if he had been cut from a block of quartz. He never told his story. He avoided those who liked to chat, preferring the company of partridges and wood pigeons in the vast shadow of the rain trees. At dawn, he roamed the streets hoping for a bit of good luck. At dusk, he wearily took any shelter offered to him out of charity. He wandered like an idle dreamer, but his nights were dreamless.

One morning, he showed a child how to write his name in the sand with a nail. They were in a wild garden where little petals filled the air like ocean spray, surrounded by flowering bushes and churned-up earth. The child had been raised on cow's milk and showed Octavio how he suckled straight from the udder and roamed the pastures without startling the beast.

For a time, the two of them were a team. In the shade of the painted houses, they stole food put out on windowsills in saucers for wild parrots. The child was quick and wily. He had a straight nose and yellow eyes, and there was something untamed about him. He climbed telegraph poles, cut the cables and collected the copper parts. He crushed beer cans under his heels and sold them on to a smelter. In bakeries, while Octavio distracted the shopkeepers' attention, the boy would stick his finger into the vats of treacle and snaffle marzipan fruits. His pockets always bore the black stain of crushed berries.

Hunger led them into graveyards. They foraged inside tombs, plundering in the darkness of vaults, finding little bronze crosses pinned to rags, mother-of-pearl rosaries and belts embellished with glass beads. Once they found a little Yanomami statue that had been turned into a lectern, holding a Bible whose pages had been devoured by vermin. They became so destitute that the moral high ground sank to their level.

Like two drunken insects, they lived for months deep in the woods of Tacarigua. While Octavio washed his clothes using guanacaste seeds, the child got lost among the bamboo, lay down and wallowed in the muddy grass and stuffed himself with green bananas until he was sick. He was more interested in flowers than people, made bouquets and wreaths, whittled canes. He sometimes disappeared for four days at a time. One night he ventured deep into the forest and never came back. He made sure to leave no trace behind him.

The separation left Don Octavio with a taste of sap and illusion. He wondered if the child had been a figment of his imagination and deep inside he sensed the bitter beauty of a world he was destined never to understand.

Alone again, he crossed the Carabobo region, travelling in the back of pick-up trucks. He helped himself to the contents of crates, ripping into watermelons with his teeth and stealing purple passion fruit wrapped in hemp. As he moved west, the grass became higher. The mountain that ran between Cabo Codera and Puerto Cabello was like an enormous grey-green muscle separating land from sea, without coves or valleys.

He reached the forests of San Esteban where the swamp led into clusters of mangroves that broke the sea up into little lagoons. Blue cranes gathered here to begin their migration towards other wetlands. Octavio headed deeper into an area of thick tree cover. The darkness beneath the canopy was like a different expression of light. He came across an old derelict building and a small patch of pasture where black donkeys came to graze.

The sandbox trees had been cut in some places: the sap was used to treat snake bites. A row of mangrove and gum trees infested with red spider mite led down to a torrent stretching twenty metres across, a tumult of foam and rocks creating an endless roar. The tropical rains had submerged the banks and made the water deep. A man could not have stood up in it.

Walls of greenery ran down both sides of the river. Don Octavio dipped his foot into the water and it bit into his ankle. He picked up a heavy branch, most likely torn from an acacia in a storm, and threw it into the water, where it spun, rebounded between the rocks, and disappeared under banks of flowering aloe.

The river was impassable at this point. Octavio walked along the bank towards a rain tree at a bend in the river. Here it opened out onto a rocky bed where the water rumbled more quietly and reached only waist height. A clay-built house with a roof of palms stood on the bank like a sentry box.

Don Octavio clapped his hands to attract attention, but no one came to the door. There were corn husks piled up by the corner of the house. He lay down in the shade of the building, but no sooner had he closed his eyes than the silence shook him awake.

The torrent had gone quiet. Only the gentle lapping of water on stone could be heard way off in the distance. He circled the house and found to his surprise that the torrent had shrunk to a trickle of water narrow enough for a child to jump over. Yet as he drew nearer, the stream began to widen and resume its deafening drumming, swelling and chattering. With every step he took, the babbling brook became more like a torrent again.

'Who are you?'

Don Octavio turned round. The man who had spoken was standing behind him dressed in a tunic like a Jesuit, and with his hair pulled back. He was long and thin, with a chest no broader than a bulrush and bones that jutted out beneath his skin in places. He was so light on his feet that he had made no sound on approaching Octavio, like a shadow.

'I'm a traveller who's lost his way,' replied Octavio.

The man took in Octavio's solid frame without a word. All at once his expression softened as an idea came into his head.

'Let's get away from the torrent,' he said at last.

They entered the house. The front door opened into a fairly bright room which smelt of wet oak and musty straw. The walls were made from a mixture of sand, clay and dung, the floor from old planks found in an abandoned shack, the windows from the windscreen of a truck. Water was brought straight from the torrent by way of a makeshift system of pipes. There was no electricity, but the house did not lack light. The hard wood of the mangrove tree had been used to build the rafters. By the entrance, hunks of meat were kept cool in a clay-walled dry well. The smell of ash wafted from a metal brazier.

'You can overcome any obstacle to get a house of your own,' the man explained with no word of introduction. 'All you need is land. With land, you have power.'

He pushed two glasses and a jug of water across a low table. Tallow candles had been stuffed into bottles and lit. An engraving of St Christopher carrying the Christ child hung behind him.

'Have we met before?' he asked.

'No.'

'Are you sure?'

'I never forget a face.'

'Nor me.'

The man was now thicker set. His cheeks had filled out and his neck had widened. He told Octavio he owned some land not far from Valencia which gave him a small income, as well as rabbits which he bartered for cloth. He said he had been a travelling salesman, a farmer and a worker on the pipelines. His life seemed to be defined by metamorphosis, to fall within a shifting outline. He had been born in a tired and barren land shunned by everyone. Now he lived off the fruits he picked, the birds he hunted, and silence.

'Well, almost silence,' he clarified; 'the torrent is always roaring away. Sometimes I hear its death rattle in the distance, only for it to come back to life.'

'Is it a torrent or a stream?'

'It's a prison.'

'What's on the other side?'

'Forests. But you need legs like tree trunks to get across. Travellers are always wanting to get to the other side. They try to throw logs across, but they end up walking the length of the bank instead. The ground is so swampy, it's been ages since anyone dared to wade across. You can drown in it.'

Don Octavio wanted to stay a few days and, without further discussion, the man hung a hammock between two breadfruit trees. Day after day, Octavio watched his curious host spend hours under the rain tree, lying flat on the grass so as not to block out any light. Every so often he would lift his head and glance at the horizon to gauge the time by the height of the sun.

Away from the water, his body was taller and stronger. At this distance he could lift beams, change the straw, carry twice his own weight. But when he approached the stream, he became visibly smaller, while the weak little stream rose up and roared once more. Don Octavio saw how the water gained the flesh the man lost as the two came together. Like two bodies sharing a common muscle, they seemed bound by the same miracle that pulled them apart again moments later.

Octavio came to like this unburdened existence. Behind the hut there was a neglected kitchen garden that had once yielded plentiful crops. The soil was loose, ploughed over and enriched with mulch, providing fertile ground for planting. Octavio offered to work the ground and grow sesame, tamarind and passion fruit. He used animal gut as a fertiliser and successfully produced lychees, custard apples and milk fruit. In the middle of the garden there was a compost heap piled into a ditch and a heavy-leafed fig tree sitting on a throne-like trunk. Octavio liked the smell of humus and foliage, the cackle of macaws in the sky, the insects swarming in the air.

One day, the torrent became so wild that it carried off a leaning tree along with a heap of branches, clumps of earth and rodent carcasses. All kinds of flotsam and jetsam washed up on the bank near the house, including a tree log which caught the owner's attention. With a blow of his axe he cut into it and stood back to consider the notch he had made in the wood.

'You see,' he said, as if reading something in the log's fibres. 'It's dry inside. It's only just been thrown into the water. We've got company.'

XI

A woman and a man skirted the edge of the forest and came to the door of the hut. They explained that they had walked upstream, thinking the torrent might prove less hostile closer to its source. They had climbed the bank and reached the top of the mountain from where they could see the sea and the islands of mangroves.

'We tried to locate the source, but we never found it,' the woman said. 'No matter how far you walk, the water keeps gushing. We threw in a log and when we saw how quickly it was carried off we decided to come down again.'

'This torrent has no source,' the host replied.

'Every river has a source.'

'It's fringed with mangroves whose seeds germinate on the tree. When they drop off, they fall at the base of the tree. Then a young mangrove begins to grow alongside its parent, pushing back the sea and wiping out the source.'

'It's only water after all,' said the woman, exasperated. 'We'll just build a raft.'

'You'll drown.'

'A bridge, then.'

'The torrent will go into spate; it's unpredictable. It'll whisk away the first plank you put across it.'

'It has to stop somewhere.'

Don Octavio, who had been following the conversation in silence, now stood up and cautiously approached the group, keeping his distance like a timid pet.

'I can get across,' he said.

The host turned round, surprised. 'What are you talking about?'

'My legs are solid enough. I know I can get across.'

'You'll drown, you fool.'

But for a moment Don Octavio's self-assurance made them forget the force of the torrent.

'I won't drown,' he replied. 'I'll tie a rope around myself. That'll make it easier.'

No sooner had he said this than he tied a rope of woven rushes and horsehair to the trunk of the rain tree. He wound the other end around his waist and loaded a wicker basket full of large stones onto his back.

'The heavier I am, the less likely I am to be swept away.'

As he came within a metre of the stream, the water seemed to swell, foaming, beating on the bank, roaring like an army. Don Octavio stepped onto a seaweed-covered rock. The torrent grew even stronger and wider, sending up mountains of water. The host threw him a staff and he managed to lean on it and find his balance before putting his other foot down. His unsteady legs withstood the force of the current, feeling their way among the pebbles to avoid the deeper parts, seeming instinctively to thwart the hidden architecture of the riverbed.

Halfway across, Octavio was almost swept away. A stone moved on the bottom, causing him to stumble. The woman let out a cry from the bank, but he soon grabbed onto the staff, regained his balance and, surprising the onlookers with his remarkable composure, fought on tirelessly. He set off again with giant steps, determined, spurred on by vigour and courage. The water buffeted his waist and the wind nipped at his neck. Still he advanced unflinchingly, battling onwards. At times, the current became so fierce that Octavio could not go on. Lashed by the all-engulfing waves, he writhed as he waited for them to subside, huddled with his arms held to his chest, before continuing with a heavy stride, his body filled with a sudden burst of energy. There he was, unbroken by battle, overcoming every danger with the boundless perseverance common to all feats of human endeavour. A storm of spray enveloped him, causing him to vanish from sight. He reappeared further on, only a metre from the opposite bank: the forest was not vast enough to hold him back.

Once on the bank, chest heaving, Octavio lay down on his stomach to catch his breath. For the first time, he could look back at the hut from the other side of the torrent. It was small and isolated. The three figures in the distance were celebrating. There was a break in the cloud; the sun struck his face and planted in his flesh the seeds of victory. And Octavio felt far and ever further away.

The crossing left a curious mark on the wood of his heart. He lost any desire to leave the hut. Instead he wished to serve that invisible master formed of foam and eddies, to hear its solitude echoed in his own. From that day on, word spread from town to town that a giant was carrying travellers across on his back in return for some food.

They came in their droves: debtors fleeing creditors, husbands fleeing wives, but also indigenous people fleeing the mines and farmers fleeing unjust landowners. Some came empty-handed, begging a favour, lambs of God. Others offered hens or pigs. Don Octavio never turned them down. This was not a case of a man becoming an animal, a beast of burden. The crossing had become essential to him because the alchemy that took place there had found its one true meaning in the rivers of his soul.

People brought him piles of smart clothes, glass-bead necklaces, *cují*-wood stools. They would place gutted hares, armadillo meat, iguana and crab eggs among the reeds, or spread out on the table squid and rainbow wrasse smelling strongly of brine. The women would take off the little gold brooches pinned to their chests and offer them to him. Don Octavio looked at these treasures, but would not touch them. As it once had been at the church, he went about his work, paying little heed to anything else.

What Octavio refused, the host accepted. He would speak knowledgeably to the self-made men and dance with folk singers, and he never confused the crosses of different parishes. Instead of his usual rags, he dressed up in delicate silks and fine woollen garments. He behaved in the manner of a gentleman, heaping compliments on the ladies. The wild vegetable garden became a neat little plot with concrete borders in which oil-rich fruits, exotic spices and pumpkins grew. Octavio grafted, tied back and watered the plants religiously so that no one leaf overshadowed another. It was a time when the wind blew in long gusts and the air was thick with butterflies. These were the early days of a civilisation, growing from community to hamlet, from hamlet to village, and from village to town. All around, life sprang from the bud of progress. Outside, the hut looked like a shack; inside, it became a palace.

The host had many mistresses. In order to give them a good welcome, he would bleed sows and dry the meat in a salt tub. He left Octavio to sleep outdoors, even when it was raining. When he was given a rifle with revolving barrels, he forgot all about the women. With childish excitement, he beat the tamarind trees with a pole to startle the sparrows and then shoot them. He neglected his vegetable garden in favour of hunting. When he headed into the forest to flush out giant coatis, it was Octavio's job to beat the drum. When he approached nests in camouflage, Octavio had to have the net ready. When the host ran out of gunpowder, he exchanged his rifle for seeds from a poacher crossing the torrent. He decided to build a watermill. He had two sandbox trees cut down to make the blades and, while he chopped off the biggest branches with a machete, Octavio built a wheel that could withstand the rising waters. But the mill never saw the light of day.

The rainy season came and the banks were covered with silt. Nobody wanted to cross any more. The flow of travellers dried up. The host would look across at the mist-shrouded forests, his eyes saying something that Octavio could not fathom. His voice crumbled to ashes. His past encounters seemed to have left him with a taste for wealth and worldly things. Now the wind brought only swirls of spray, not music or flowers.

With no meat available, they had to make do with seeds. The soil became infested with larvae and the vegetable garden yielded nothing but dry roots. As the water flooded the furrows, the earth turned to bog. The fig tree died in the space of a few sorry days. Iguanas with scaly tails and amber eyes came down from the trees to eat what remained of the last shoots. The wind dislodged the grafts and blew down the arbours. Empty of butterflies, the nights fell without dusk.

The host spoke of emigrating to the city. He harked back to the good life he had known only yesterday, the food he had tasted, the women he had kissed. He constantly fought off memories, his heart full of disappointment. Within days, he was plagued by nightmares. He would wake with a start, talking of horned monsters that looked like devils, his sweat tasting of the torrent. Sobs quivered in his throat, but would not come out. Don Octavio made him infusions of nettles and cinnamon and purges that took away his appetite, and bled him until he became dozy. The host got worse, sinking into delirium, sweating profusely, eyes rolling.

One morning, panic-stricken by a vision, he woke Don Octavio and pointed wordlessly at the other bank. For the first time, Octavio caught the whiff of rotten flesh on him. He stood up, lifted the host onto his shoulders and waded into the torrent.

The waves let out a mad, deep moan. As Octavio moved forward, the torrent rammed into him. The host's muscles shrank, his skeleton grew thinner, and Octavio felt him weakening, growing limper as they went. And yet, with each step, the load grew heavier. The host had stopped speaking now, and was gurgling like a baby. His legs dangled on either side of Octavio's neck, and his hands waved in midair. The years were falling away from him.

A few metres from the bank, Octavio turned. What he saw, surrounded by a mysterious light, was a beautiful, smiling child, pure and white, who, for a split second, seemed to carry on his back the unbearable weight of all men. The child pointed at the bank with his fat, tiny little finger. The battle of the waves was ending. The host was no longer the host, but a trace of himself. The torrent had swallowed up his life, a life whose weakness possibly gave the river a fragile beauty it had previously lacked.

By the end of the crossing, of the two men, only one remained.

XII

From that day on, Octavio's journey was no longer that of a mendicant. There was something pure about his wanderings that seemed to inspire others to blindly follow him. His turmoil at the host's demise soon gave way to a fresh burst of curiosity. He did not leave the forest of San Esteban, but roamed the hamlets that lined the motorway to Morón.

Along the edge of the forest between Las Trincheras and El Cambur, he found villages so isolated there was no postal service. Wherever he went, he brought rich harvests, bumper crops and news of neighbouring hamlets. He walked the streets among the cats and goats, ankle-deep in mud, wearing light clothing with a bag of achenes and nuts tied to his belt. He carried two chicken legs over his shoulder, half eaten, the rest salted to feed a mouth other than his own.

He encountered evangelical preachers who exploited farmers' superstitions for their gain, and black seers who made enigmatic gestures and read fortunes in seashells. But Don Octavio had no need of religious education, of Santería or Gnosticism. He needed no altar to pray before or square to preach in. He went from house to house offering his services, repairing the wall of an infirmary or the roof of a school. With the help of other men, he carried out his good works, lay electricity cables along roads, put up fences in fields, and once, beside a barn, single-handedly castrated a bull no one else would go near.

He no longer stole from cemeteries; he built walls, weeded out niches and helped to fill in the graves. He slept in grain stores on a white baize sheet. He lived free of worry, knowing he would win back tomorrow what he lost today. He spent his richest hours in the service of the poor.

Women wanted him for their son; girls, for their husband. The hill at El Dique was bequeathed to him. Octavio continued on his way. As he walked, he felt an almost poetic devotion to the world. Some talked of a giant born of a torrent, others of a slave who had claimed his freedom. People asked where he came from and he told them: the earth.

He reached a cluster of homes encircled by trees. Beyond the village, the land sloped down to a river where tilapia were farmed in a small clay pool. The community was made up of indigenous families and Creoles who had tacitly agreed to live side by side in wattle-and-daub huts that stood on a large circle of rammed earth, separated by straw fences. During the day, men with goatee beards brought in the harvest, never looking up from their work, while the women treated asthma with seje oil and eczema with orange latex. Workers in espadrilles gleaned the wheat and, in the heart of the village, children were thrashed with violet lantana branches to drive off chickenpox.

Octavio stayed a few months. Illiteracy had cut the village off from the world. In the absence of teachers, the villagers could read only the whims of the sky and count to fifty. Since he knew nothing of the laws of pedagogy and had no example to go by, Octavio saw no reason why he should not attempt to impart the basics of the alphabet. Every weekday morning in a *churuata* that also served as sleeping quarters, infirmary and marketplace, a gaggle of indigenous and Creole children awaited him, playing rowdy games of catch on the sun-drenched road until they saw Don Octavio's strong and solid frame loom on the blazing horizon.

A strict, hard-working man, he soon taught his students to follow his example. The girls learnt to write through dictation and the boys to count a tree's fruits at a single glance. When children missed class to make hay or tend their flocks, Octavio let them off, telling himself they were learning nature's lessons instead.

As a reward for his dedication, the adults of the village offered to build Octavio a hut beside a millrace fed by water that could be drunk. Octavio saw in this little channel an allegory of the torrent that had driven the host mad. He told the villagers he would find his own lodgings and took the path towards the summit of the Hilaria range, a few kilometres away.

Rain was falling in heavy bursts. Octavio climbed until he reached a tall and shabby wall.

Bare-headed in the rain, he sheltered under some low-hanging branches beside the wall. As darkness fell, he decided to spend the night there. He pulled aside hanging white trumpets of bindweed, cut down the plants that twisted round the stones, and scraped away humus and weeds. He gathered up twigs and built a hearth in a circle of pebbles. The first flames kindled the leaves and he blew on them to get the fire going. But as the flickers lit his surroundings, he suddenly saw a huge purple rock four or five metres high bearing down on him from all sides like some drunken monster. Three great scars ran across it and the stone was covered in drawings that seemed to stare at him from a distance of a million years.

There were images of insects, stars, animals and tools. Octavio began to try to decipher the symbols. The mute stone spoke every language. It took him a few minutes to recognise a detail from the Campanero carving – the stone that had led to all these months of exile since the night of the burglary, the stone whose only readers should have been the macaws and the orchids.

He saw that the symbols were arranged almost geometrically. There was a coherence to the whole – the groups of animals were distinct from the group of stars; the mysterious object conformed to a simple architecture. Yet the writing had not been drawn by human hand. Thousands of forms of plant life had eaten into the cold nourishment of stone, covering the ground with moss and every cranny with ferns, claiming rightful ownership. Thus, at Campanero, writing was not born of man, but of the irrational power of nature and its unimpeded tropical, crazy thirst to spread, to grow ever taller and wider. It was born of a frenzy beyond all excess, the salt smell of the ocean on the wind, the shape of Hilaria's mighty peak; it was born here, amid the mountains along the coast of Venezuela and the soundless forests of San Esteban.

The jungle protected its relics. A circle of trees rose around the stone to shade the drawings and prevent them from tanning in the sun. The place was far from the capuchin monkeys who might have rubbed against it and wiped away the marks. The air was filled with foliage that protected the stone from toucan droppings. Nature jealously guarded her heritage, surrounding it with rosewood and kapok trees, ceibas, giant interlaced creepers and ball-shaped, long-spined cactuses. Like a mother, nature defended her offspring. She had not seen men like Guerra or the brotherhood of burglars coming. Amid the lively clamour of indigenous languages, she gave birth to hieroglyphics drawn from organic depths, murmuring and moving in Campanero.

Octavio knelt before the fire, hugged his knees to his chest and remained crouching in the half-light.

The light of the fire cast the shadow of his hands onto the walls, repeating his gestures. To see him, anyone would know for certain he was descended from an animal in a cave drawing.

All of humanity was contained within him. Octavio was finally witnessing the birth of a literature he had long searched for on the shelves of the church and in Venezuela's lessons. The great book had been closed for a thousand years, resisting the ravages of time like the stone. And so literature was itself a stone.

XIII

In the village, there were two huts one hundred metres apart, one belonging to the Reyes, the other to the Atalayas. The two families traded with one another, kept within their boundaries and prevented their animals from straying onto their neighbour's land. The differing customs that should traditionally have been a barrier between them had, by force of habit, become what bound them.

Zoilo Reyes, the father, was a cold and unpleasant man, as hard as nails, whose passion for collecting had led him to accumulate all kinds of useless objects. Though his hut was small and low-ceilinged, it resembled a hardware shop where village people came to browse and buy, even on a Sunday. He kept untidy records of scribbled-down dates and incidents, hoping his tiny observations might feed the miracles of science and invention of tomorrow. Everything in this living museum smelt of genever and fish oil.

He and his wife, Ana María Reyes Sánchez, had seventeen children, the youngest of whom, Eva Rosa, had shone from her earliest years. Eva Rosa helped to farm the fish, wove bags from goat hair, trimmed the cows' hooves with maternal care and was up sowing corn before sunrise. She had a face like a china doll, pale little metallic-grey eyes, and delicate skin as yet untouched by age. She always wore a tortoiseshell comb in her hair and wrapped her centimos in a hankie hidden inside her bra, so as to keep her fortune close to her heart. Yet there came a time when modest, sensible Eva Rosa, who never indulged in gossip, became the talk of the town herself.

She had secretly fallen in love with the baby of the Atalaya family, Chinco – a dark, handsome, slightly sad-looking indigenous boy – the day he had given her a little birdcage he had made out of teak branches. Chinco Atalaya was a hard-working, honest lad. His skin was like powdered red ochre. He was quiet and a little mysterious, respectful towards all things and all people, and the way he could plough a straight furrow, harness a horse, trim a hedge and graft a rosebush was undeniably erotic.

That day, the pair set off together into the fields with flowers clinging to their hair, searching every nest they came across for a troupial for their cage. It was a warm day. Eva Rosa was wearing a light dress and laughing at everything. Chinco Atalaya took her hand shyly but firmly. His adolescent face glowed with the light of things to come. They made their way slowly through the woods, larking about, rolling in the undergrowth, opening their hearts, urging each other on. And as their laughter was hushed in the grassy hollow, they knew the cage would never be big enough to contain all the wild birds of their desires, and they shed their feathers in a flurry of kisses.

When she was six weeks late, Eva Rosa realised she was pregnant. Since Zoilo had brought his children up to believe that women, like animals, should not produce offspring until their prime years of hard graft were over, she tried several times to abort the baby using leeks pulled from the fields that, like sponges, emerged from her body soaked as purple as aubergines.

By December, Eva Rosa could no longer hold in her belly. When Zoilo found out, he stormed into the hut, searched the piles of bric-a-brac for the rifle he always kept clean and oiled, and set off to kill his daughter for having broken the family rules. Seeing her father draw his gun, in an act of self-preservation, Eva Rosa closed a door as the shot rang out. And so in the end the only punishment she received for her original sin was a splinter that struck her as the bullet hit the door with a guilty clamour.

Everyone in the village told a different version of the story. A few days later, it was Zoilo who came to apologise as humbly as an apostle and drew a veil over the whole business by hanging a handsome blue ivory crucifix right over the bullet hole.

At some point around March, Eva Rosa began to scream at the top of her voice as her contractions started. The village women lay the girl on a large upturned wicker trunk inside the Atalayas' hut, the floor of which had been lined with dry grass. She was surrounded by a ring of girls in white dresses who wrung out red towels and placed damp cloths over her face in almost total darkness. Her mother, Ana María Reyes Sánchez, who was also pregnant, handed enamel jugs that smelt of balsam to a man whose face was barely visible in the gloom.

He was wearing striped trousers, a baseball cap and a beige gilet with lots of zipped pockets. He looked as if he came from the city. A large bag lay open at his side containing antiseptics, compresses, rehydration sachets, sweet almond oil for cradle cap, and condoms. The only illumination came from a few tallow candles. Standing between Eva Rosa's bloodied thighs in the barely lit room, he seemed to be bringing the child into the world with only the girl's contractions and screams to guide him.

The labour lasted three days. Outside, Zoilo paced breathlessly up and down, anxiously kicking tin cans. Several times he had to be held back from entering the hut by two mulattos. On the second day, after rifling through his assorted junk, he found a tent which he put up opposite the Atalayas' hut and he camped there among the peasants, ready for anything. As the third day dawned, the women emerged from the hut. Zoilo shoved his way to the front of the crowd with his arms held out to receive the child, yet to his surprise, the midwives placed twins there: one with Eva

Rosa's fair skin; the other, Chinco's duller complexion. Moved as never before, Zoilo's voice quavered.

'They're like the sun and the moon!' he said at last. 'May heaven protect them!'

Crying enough tears for three, he announced he would do all he could to give them a wonderful childhood and, cradling a boy in each arm, he returned to his hut where a lifelong bond with these two children awaited him – the very same children he had tried to kill just a few months earlier.

The family took care of Eva Maria as she recovered from the birth. Neighbours helped to clear up and wash the floor. A crowd of well-wishers came and went. As Octavio thrust his way through, he heard someone call out behind him.

'Don Octavio!'

He turned round. The man in the baseball cap and beige gilet who had spent three days on the receiving end of Eva Rosa's cries was Alberto Perezzo, the young doctor from San Pablo del Limón. Smelling strongly of disinfectant and smoke, he held out long arms covered in blood.

'You're a new man, Octavio!' he gushed. 'Had your hands placed in the wounds of Christ, or what?'

He was laughing. He spoke with the accent of the capital. The doctor put his arms around Octavio in an outpouring of warmth, and Octavio saw for the first time how this familiar gesture could immediately close the distance between doctor and patient. Exhausted from his work, Perezzo was slowly taking in what he had seen.

'Sad, isn't it?' he said. 'Two kids of sixteen and fourteen with two kids of their own. That makes four mouths to feed. Not ideal conditions in which to bring up children.'

'They'll work it out.'

'Well, they haven't got much choice ...'

'There's always a choice,' Octavio replied sagely.

The young doctor stepped back to take a better look at him. Octavio had changed. He was in control of his body. It was clear from the way he held himself with his shoulders thrust back.

They sat down beside the tilapia pond, which was covered in shimmering white blankets of weed. Where the pond narrowed, a channel flowed off it. The young doctor rolled up his sleeves, scrubbed his arms with pink soap and splashed himself clean. He had lost weight, but there was still the same look of determination on his face. He glanced at Octavio sitting beside him with his hands flat on his knees. Though he appeared calm, Octavio was not quite at ease.

'Doctor, what are you doing here?'

Alberto Perezzo took a moment before replying. He mopped the beads of sweat from his brow and started scrubbing his arms again, leaning over the water. The question seemed to have thrown him.

'Things have taken a turn for the worse in San Pablo,' he began. 'There was some kind of raid on the church; I'm not sure exactly what it was about. Everyone says something different. I spend all my time with the sick ... and because they're stuck indoors, they end up with a distorted view of things.'

He said this to soften the blow, but Octavio, who knew nothing of the custom of treading carefully, did not visibly react. The water was making a pounding noise like a stone.

'I don't know any more than the next person,' the doctor went on. 'I heard the church had been overrun with burglars, thieves, something like that. There was a raid, anyway. I, for one, decided it was time to pack my bags.'

He fell silent, fearing he had said too much. He didn't wish to talk about the shoot-outs that had set the barrio ablaze, the half-collapsed church, the injured women, the militias who had got involved to protect their own interests, or the police firing from behind the walls. He didn't wish to discuss it with Octavio, who had distanced himself from that world and sown another one with walnut trees, mallows and mimosas, filled with simple country folk, children cutting down branches to make handles for tools and women carrying eggs in their aprons.

'Whatever the truth of it,' said the doctor, 'it has given me the chance to see some other parts of the country, which is no bad thing! Not for you either, Octavio.'

'No, indeed.'

'I took a flying boat from Puerto Ayacucho to San Fernando de Atabapo. I worked for two months at a clinic in María Garrido. Makes a change from Caracas. Did you know nature provides a cure for every illness it creates? Honestly ... you have no idea how many prescriptions the forest provides!'

Don Octavio said 'I know' and 'exactly' so breezily that Alberto Perezzo soon realised he wasn't listening. Using the toe of his sandal, he was drawing lines, shapes and his initials in the sand. The water in front of them refracted the light. It flowed, solid and constant, to the other end of the country, all the way to the one hundred mouths of the Orinoco on the Paria Peninsula, carrying with it all the scents of San Esteban, all the roars of Macarao, all the tongues of Tacarigua. Its gentle progress, like his own, mingled with the promise of exile.

Seeing Octavio so downhearted, the doctor tried to end on an optimistic note.

'But, you know, it's not all bad in the barrio. The church has been put on a list of heritage sites to be restored. They want to turn it into a theatre.'

Octavio jumped at these words.

'A theatre?'

'Yes,' replied the doctor, 'as part of a programme to reclaim public spaces.'

Octavio stared towards the horizon and fell to contemplation. Unsettled, he mumbled to himself, 'Why a theatre?'

Thinking the question was meant for him, Alberto Perezzo looked down at his reddened arms and eventually said, 'True. They could have turned it into a delivery room.'

XIV

The idea of leaving came to Don Octavio quietly and straight-forwardly, as plain as fact. The long journey he had already taken suddenly seemed to catch up with him, weighing heavily on him. His tall frame began to hunch a little. If he must leave again, he thought to himself, it should be for the last time. And so the courage and tenacity that had made it possible for him to wander for so long in the lands of San Esteban now also made it possible for him to return to San Pablo del Limón over the course of a few exhausting days.

He thought he wouldn't recognise the place he had left in such a hurry. On the bus to Caracas, he saw the countryside he had taken two years to cross now pass before his eyes in the space of two days. He was dropped at La Bandera, from where he took another bus to San Pablo.

He wandered aimlessly through the jungle of alleyways, some so narrow you had to approach them sideways on. Gone were the endless expanses of countryside, the vast fields, the open plateaux that stretched for kilometres. Now the space was divided by lines of concrete with boarding houses that spread over several floors, cubes of brick piled on top of one another like insect nests. The corridors smelt of straw mattresses and crushed mangoes. At the foot of a flight of stairs, a lone beggar held a sign that read: 'Please give generously to the national heritage of poverty.' Everything seemed hopeless. Octavio's head was spinning. Yet in spite of the filth and the danger, this was his barrio, the land he was born in, the deep and stony ground he had grown up on. Plunged into a nostalgia he could barely explain, he felt something approaching tenderness.

He climbed up the hill, wanting to see his house again. Against the walls of his hovel, he found shovelfuls of rubbish, nettles and a cesspool stinking of urine. A hen was pecking at breadcrumbs by a low wall. He could hear a conversation through the door.

He knocked. The voices went quiet.

'Who's there?'

He knocked again.

The door was opened by a tall, stout woman built like a barrel, with rollers in her hair. She was wiping her hands on a hairdressing apron. She was used to looking down at men, but Octavio was a good head taller than her. She went weak at the knees at the sight of him, but was soon making light of it.

'*Cristo*,' she said. 'I'd rather feed you than dress you!'

Laughter could be heard from inside the house and the voice from before asked again, 'Who is it?' less loudly but more insistently this time.

The woman's rollers bobbed on her head. She shamelessly looked Octavio up and down and, leaning back into the sitting room, replied, 'You can stop looking for a husband to support you, sweetheart … I've found you a tree that'll put you in the shade.'

Then, eyeing Octavio closely, she invited him to follow her, swinging her hips as she went.

Makeshift shelves had been put up in the overfilled living room to house bits of old rubbish, crockery and packets of bread flour. There were pleasant cooking smells in the air. A younger woman was sitting beside a table. She had hairpins tucked into her dressing gown and was blowing on her nails to dry the polish. When she saw Octavio come in, she pulled her dressing gown up around her neck and, looking a little worried, asked for the third time, 'Will somebody please tell me who this is?'

Octavio put his things down.

'I'm the man who lived here before.'

'Before what?' the woman asked haughtily.

He didn't answer. Looking around the room, he recognised the table, which still had traces of charcoal on it. The partition dividing the two rooms was still standing and the bedroom door was closed. As he scoured every detail of the room, the taller woman held on to the back of the chair and said, as if she had already tried and failed to make herself clear, 'If you're new here, I know someone who can find you a bed. I can rent you an electricity meter. There are wires hanging out of it like a creeper. But, Señor …' she said, turning serious, 'this is our place now.'

Without any deeds to the property, Don Octavio knew he had no chance of getting his house back. The land had never really been his. As he picked up his bundle of belongings and made to leave, he heard a groan like a death rattle coming from the bedroom, a long, loud cry of pain. The woman in rollers did not react. A second moan shattered the moment, and Octavio put down his things.

'I'd like to see the bedroom one last time,' he said.

'It's private,' she said in a tone that admitted no further discussion.

'Señorita,' he said defensively, 'I've lived here all my life.'

Huffing irritably, the woman stopped protesting, stomped over to the bedroom door and yanked it open. Inside, there was a bed, a wardrobe and a chair. The little altar had been turned into a bedside table with a radio sitting on top of it.

Octavio stepped inside the room. Something stirred between

the bed and the wall. A dog must be sleeping under the bed. But as the shape moved and became clearer, he saw it was a young man, probably in his twenties, who stood up, his face puffy and wrists bound. His foot was attached to the bottom of the wardrobe by a long chain. Both men jumped. They considered one another in the dim light like two animals locked in a wordless exchange.

The man brought his hand to his side and gasped in pain. The chain clinked with every step he took. He had long hair, a thin body and red eyes. His trousers were stained with trails of blood. His breathing was laboured and uneven. He seemed to have been left in this prison for days without medical or loving care.

'What is that ...' Octavio could not help mumbling.

The woman went blank, looking at the boy with a mixture of pride and sacrifice.

'That ...' she said, 'is my son.'

'Why's he chained up?' Octavio asked, outraged.

'So they don't kill him,' she replied, her voice catching in her throat.

Octavio had no wish to hear more, and the woman did not elaborate. There was no anger or suffering in her eyes, but they shone with Virginal splendour. Perhaps it was she who was truly enchained. And Octavio saw burning in her gaze a secret resemblance to the forests of San Esteban.

Hoisting his bundle onto his shoulder, he hurried out, passing the girl on his way and stopping to announce bluntly, 'I'd like my table back.'

The woman in rollers nodded her consent. She told the girl to clear away her nail polish and make-up. Bread had been broken over this table; it had been sewn and ironed on; dough had been kneaded, onions sliced; tears of grief had fallen on it. New scars shone on its surface. Octavio lifted it onto his back and this time it felt heavier to him. He went the way he used to go, his back bent, his heart full of splinters, leaving his days of ignorance and solitude behind him, leaving the house that was no longer his.

XV

The church restoration works began in June and went on until the following August. The architect in charge was a man from Valera, Temístocles Jerez, who had been born in the ashes of the state of Trujillo and had helped to restore the Mario-Briceño-Irragory Library and the Teatro Municipal de Caracas. He was obese, with very white skin and very black gelled curls, known for his colourful Spanish and rhetorical flourishes. He was referred to as *Doctor* despite having dropped out of university midway through his course, and he smelt of sweet *currunchete*. He had shaved off his beard in an effort to attract women, but still found himself trying to stroke it out of habit when deep in thought.

He had come up the slope to the restoration site with the foreman, Bracamonte, in a handcart filled with materials. The ground around the church was yellow and rocky and strewn with rubbish. Bracamonte looked up to assess the state of the roof joists and took measurements. Using a chisel, he made a groove between the stones of a collapsed section of wall.

'The pointing is crumbling, and there's only an old wooden frame holding up the walls,' he observed, roughly calculating the solidity of timber and pillars. 'It needs steel reinforcements.'

Temístocles Jerez always wrote everything down in a little notebook so he wouldn't have to worry about it later. He noted down 'steel reinforcements' and moved on to the topic of sanding.

He explained that the façade must be preserved in keeping with the neoclassical style but, given the pollution levels in the city, advised replacing the white paint with a granite colour. He talked of props and supports for load-bearing walls. He asked Bracamonte to look for leaks in the roof and then had two workers force open the door.

Under the fragile arches of the nave, everything was in disarray. There was a huge mountain of prayer benches piled up on top of one another, and the scent of regret hung in the air. Ripples of light came in through broken stained-glass windows and fell on the rough plaster walls. The ceiling was caving in and birds of prey had made their nests in the gabled roof frame.

Temístocles lifted up his little notebook. 'Panelling: highly flammable … replace with bent aluminium.' A niche housing a statue of the Virgin seemed like the perfect spot for the box office. With his fingers, he peeled off a flake of paint that had been hanging to the right of the doorway. He took out his notebook and crossed out the last entry. 'Before the aluminium,' he wrote, 'strip off lead paint.'

Behind the altar, he noticed a little bolted door, slightly below floor level. He pushed the lock gently with his foot, imagining the strike plate to be fragile, but it did not budge. He tried harder, pushing back against the altar table: the bolt was well and truly stuck and the door would not give. He slid a crowbar between the wall and the lock, but as he was preparing to lever it, Bracamonte called him from outside.

The top of the demolition crane was too wide for the narrow alleyways and could not get between the tightly packed houses. Temístocles felt his head spin with all the unexpected hiccups that lay ahead. He asked Bracamonte to send the crane back, told the workers to unload the demolition tools and, when everyone was gone, he sat down on a prayer bench and wrote in his notebook in a burst of inspiration, 'Ad augusta per angusta'.

From then on, they avoided heavy machinery in favour of

easily transportable tools that could be put together on the spot. Work started at the beginning of the week. A truck stopped at the bottom of the hill and the workmen unloaded tiles, beams, bricks and fibreglass. They used the garden with the pomegranate trees as an assembly area. While the builders put up the scaffolding, the joiners worked elbow to elbow trimming planks, driving in wedges and planing wood on their workbenches. The carpenters climbed ladders to plug leaks by nailing slats of wood between the roof tiles.

At the sight of the ruined church, passers-by stopped to look and give their opinion or walk off in protest. Standing among them, Don Octavio felt no trace of nostalgia. On the contrary, he was fascinated by this display of human alchemy and the quiet pride of the men who had replaced the burglars. He decided to try his luck.

They offered him a labouring job, paid at a piece rate. His role was to bring materials to the building site, clear up rubbish, empty skips and move planks. He was given a hatchet with which to cut up the old plaster and square off blocks of stone.

His job was simple but the other workers were in awe of the way he went about it. He had more stamina and strength than several machines put together. He distributed the weight he was carrying evenly in order to remain steady on his feet, knew how to use a trowel and break things down with a mallet. He worked as quickly by hand as a cement mixer. With his neck and arms covered in sweat, he embodied an animal strength that pushed forward blindly, unthinkingly, his breathing regular, recovering more quickly than others. Temístocles Jerez himself was rendered almost speechless the day he looked down from the wooden balcony and saw Octavio shiny with sweat under the lights, laden with a dozen bags of lime that three ordinary men could not have carried between them, as if he had nothing but a bundle of wheat on his back.

At lunchtime, workers took off their hard hats and ate on site, sitting on stacks of wood among the planes and saws. There was no chatting; their minds emptied by work, they silently passed a bottle of grain spirit among them. After a short siesta, the carpenter got up, the joiner went back to his wood, the builders woke the labourers, and the whole silent crowd kept on like the anvil under the hammer of hard labour. Octavio was struck by this industrious scene in which every man was as distinct and necessary as a word in the music of a sentence.

Those who were paid extra to patrol the site set up beds to sleep there. They lay their foam mattresses on the bare ground and installed a TV which could only receive one channel. At night, Octavio wandered the church alone, keeping watch as he had done before, in his thirty years of servitude, in order to protect another treasure.

One evening, while inspecting inside the building, he noticed a bolted door, slightly below floor level, whose lock appeared to have been forced. He leant against it and it gave way, opening into a small side room whose only source of daylight was a window at floor level.

A large number of sculptures had been hidden away here. Stepping inside, he saw porphyry vases, plaster monks and golden blowpipes. Behind a small stack of maple chairs was an inlaid Algerian thuya piano on top of which a pair of candelabras and some silver coffee pots gathered dust. A Veracruz hammock hung between the beams, concealing the back of the room. He made out a black lacquered chest of drawers covered in eggshell mosaic, two mirrored console tables and a set of blue stone adzes. Guerra's treasure had been left untouched.

Pushing the chairs out of his way and drawing the hammock to one side, he saw hidden under a white sheet at the back of the room the statue of the Nazarene of St Paul shining like never before in the pale-purple light. The scent of processions still seemed to hang around it. The heavy black walnut cross rested on its right shoulder, which was draped in a mantle. Dried orchids hung from its chasuble and a crown of thorns gave the top of its head a spring-like air. Though stooped and leaning, the statue was built to last centuries, dominating the room.

Octavio moved closer, holding on to the hammock as the shadows became dense. Reaching out his hand, he was two, perhaps three centimetres from the statue when his foot became caught in the fabric of the hammock, the beam from which it was hanging opened up like a fruit and the whole structure of the building came crashing down.

The collapse of the church woke the workers with a start. It took several men to clear a path to the little door, which had been blocked by the splintered beam. Panicking, they pushed their way through to find Octavio's body lying beneath a pile of bricks and rubble, his arm pinned to the floor by the wreckage. In spite of the tight space inside the tiny room, the men joined together to form a human chain and the heap of rubble gradually reduced. When Octavio felt a crack opening up in the stones above him, he drew back his arm like a wounded dog. He tucked it inside his jacket without taking the time to examine it, and fled the church.

XVI

The discovery of the side room meant that the first inventory of props could be drawn up. Everything that had survived the collapse of the building was logged on the books of the new theatre, registered as national patrimony, and put at the set designers' disposal. But the recovered artworks were in a sorry state: statues were turning to dust, paintings were falling out of their frames and tabletops were unsteady on their legs. Specialist restorers were called in, arriving in the neighbourhood on the main road. They demanded foreign products, wielded acids willy-nilly and cut corners every step of the way. Within hours they had given up and were on their way again.

Amid the comings and goings, Octavio reappeared, his arm bandaged up to the elbow. The building site had felt his absence keenly. As he was no longer up to working outdoors, he was assigned the job of maintaining the interior. After clearing out the rubbish, throwing stones into skips and piling debris into sacks, he took it upon himself to clean every item that had been catalogued.

The tableware had been dulled by dust and humidity. He recognised tin by weight, silver by smell. He scraped ochre off the building and mixed it with washing powder and oil to make a polishing paste. He treated light marks with ether and ingrained stains with warmed talc. The antiquarians had left turps, pine tar and whiting piled up in a corner. For the first time in his life, Octavio was able to read the labels.

Someone told him the best way to get rid of spots on glass was with a knob of butter, another advised him to clean the paintings with slices of onion. Bracamonte claimed that a mixture of freshly slaked lime and ox-blood serum was all that was needed to treat chestnut. Octavio set to work making concoctions. In the absence of brimstone, he would polish the carvings with antimony; lacking cuttlefish bones, he buffed the reliefs with pumice.

When he saw the results, Temístocles Jerez encouraged Octavio to keep going. He pointed out several old pieces of abandoned furniture at the back of the side room, their legs and crosspieces riddled with woodworm. Octavio made identical pieces at his workbench, replaced them and sealed them. Using two glasses of potassium per litre of water, he applied a greyish foam to the tables and chairs as they lay on their backs, rinsing off the crystals with a fine-spouted watering can. To dry them off, he would sprinkle over wood bleach, which gave the oak a lovely golden sheen. The upholstery fabric was often fringed, which sometimes made it difficult to tidy up. Octavio would run a razor blade carefully along the edge and stick it back down with glue.

The labourers gazed at the wonder of static electricity as Octavio rubbed amber with a woollen cloth. They saw how, after painting pieces of potash with distemper, the solder came together. They lavished compliments on Octavio, heaping words of praise on him that made him blush. He brushed off any suggestion that he was some kind of scientist. He simply got back to work without a word, burnishing bronze, polishing ivory and buffing up lock fittings. As he worked on his adornments, he cloaked himself in silence.

Temístocles Jerez often came into the side room, knocking on the door and opening it soundlessly to find Octavio standing in the half-light at the back of the room. He had the devoted air of a saint in a stained-glass window. He wore a large apron with a chisel, a veneer saw, a ruler and several scrubbing brushes sticking out of the front pocket. He ate on his own and worked through the night. Though bent by his humble condition, he revelled in the grandeur of his task. Watching him, Temístocles seemed to understand the mystery of servitude, from which this giant drew his strength.

'How's your arm?' he asked.

Octavio's arm was bound in a handkerchief. He spoke only when spoken to.

'Strong as an oak.'

And with that he returned to his work.

Around November, he was asked to tidy up the statue of the Nazarene of St Paul, which had fallen into a pitiful state not so much because of the disaster at the church as through years of neglect. Woodworm had eaten into the reliefs and the face had been scorched by church candles and covered in various drips and traces of mastic. The collapse of the building had ripped off one of its arms, which now lay close to the window.

Octavio began by injecting insecticide into the heart of the statue. Then he diluted some wood filler with acetone to make it the consistency of runny honey and proceeded to touch up the statue, tending to the cracks in the wood. Having no gold to hand, he made up a mixture of white lead, gypsum and ash. He repaired the bells using tissue paper and an iron. He spent entire days heating sand to fill gaps. He used shellac on the burr wood and stuck missing pieces back on to match the grain. He removed ink stains with household hydrochloric acid and blood with sodium thiosulphate. He touched up the paintwork with gouache and polished it with virgin beeswax. At last he gilded the crown of thorns, but only on one side; since it was to be used as a prop on stage, it would only be seen from the front.

The rainy season came, the cool December wind turning to fat drops of rain which made the ground boggy, running with filthy streams. Long showers washed the sky. From time to time the sun appeared and the stifling heat quickly dried the theatre's boards.

In spite of the bad weather, Temístocles Jerez came to check up on the works regularly, accompanied by an official from the town hall. One day, he appeared alongside a straight-backed man in a panama hat and white linen jacket. Though he looked like a tourist, it was clear that he was also a man of the world.

Without touring the church, they headed straight for the side room where Octavio was working, his face buried in the gloom. They paid no more attention to him than they would have to a painting. Outside, the rain was pelting down. Temístocles' mind went blank.

'Señor …?' he asked his companion apologetically.

'Señor Paz,' the man replied.

Temístocles cleared his throat and turned to Octavio.

'Señor Paz has all the necessary paperwork to reclaim the statue of the Nazarene. Apparently it was stolen from his apartment by the burglars who used to operate out of the church.'

'Real brutes,' the man added emphatically.

At the sound of his voice, Octavio spun round. Beneath the straw hat, he saw a man of average size with a round, high-coloured face hidden behind dark glasses. Something about him was familiar. The man looked Octavio straight in the eye: Guerra did not blink.

Guerra had disguised himself as a cabinet-maker living in Indonesia. He claimed to be a connoisseur of Venezuelan art forced to retreat to a more stable market by the country's political troubles. He collected ivory virgins, blood-drenched figures of Christ and giltwood depictions of heaven, but his real weakness was for processional statues.

Octavio said nothing. Guerra held out his hand to seal the deal, and Temístocles felt a sudden surge of friendship towards him.

'I'm amazed you came such a long way for a simple wooden statue, Señor Paz. Jakarta, was it?'

'It's where my business interests are,' he replied completely naturally. 'You see, I'm sentimental enough to be rather attached to this statue. It reminds me that wherever we are in the world, we Venezuelans remain the children of myth.'

'Of myth?'

The side room was minuscule; their mouths were practically touching. Pointing at the damage from the accident, he explained: 'Yes, of myth, absolutely. Every people has its original wound: ours is the collapse of our history. In order to rebuild it, we've had to turn to myth. More or less what happened to the Greeks too, I might add.'

'I'm an architect,' Temístocles replied, enjoying the exchange. 'I don't know much about the Pyramids.'

Guerra smiled and made to leave, but the architect, reluctant to let the conversation drop, was moving on to more general reflections on Antiquity. Determined to continue the discussion, he raised his game, opening the conversation out to encompass how stone was formed and the likely age of civilisation.

'You're an architect,' Guerra cut in. 'You know perfectly well that the Pyramids weren't built by us. Our kings didn't create states. Our princes didn't build walls. Historically, Venezuela has merely been a country for empires to pass through. A "*por ahora*" country, a country for the time being. Colonial structures, government buildings, military academies: none of them were built for the future, none carry any memory of the past. It was all put up *por ahora* … The conquistadors moved in *por ahora* before carrying on down to Potosí where the richest mines were … stopping by *por ahora* before founding the viceroyalties of Colombia ... before opening up the countryside to the multinationals.'

Temístocles Jerez showed his assent with 'exactly' and 'that's right', captivated by the political turn the discussion was taking.

'Nothing has ever been properly finished,' Guerra went on. 'This is a bivouac country. I'm not telling you anything you don't already know. Didn't you just destroy a church? So of course we had to turn to myth, make up a story instead of a history. And what's come of it?'

'Theatre!' cried Temístocles.

He followed his remark with a throaty laugh that echoed off the vaulted ceiling. Guerra merely smiled.

'No, Señor Jerez. What has come of it is this.'

He pointed to the statue.

'That's our pyramid. That's our Greeks. No regime, no occupation, no show of riches can take it from us. When we carry that statue, we carry the earth itself.'

On the architect's orders, Octavio took the Nazarene to the back of a pick-up truck that Guerra had parked outside the church. Its head stuck out above the cabin. He attached the arms, stood it on its stand and rolled up the purple mantle to protect it from the building dust. The truck drove off. For the last time, Octavio glimpsed the outline of the saint through the exhaust fumes. Tall and sturdy with a strong back and thick hands, it left the theatre bound and gagged like a pig in a pushcart, feet scraping against the wheels as it was dragged through the middle of a faithless age.

XVII

When the struts and scaffolds began to come down at the beginning of August, for the first time the dazzling new theatre was revealed to everyone. Perhaps some who saw it understood the building's historic importance. A government delegation came to see how work was progressing. Temístocles Jerez proudly showed off the roof renovations and the new flooring in the passageways backstage.

The stage itself had been fitted with a mechanism which, like the capstan of a ship, could make the wings retract and be replaced with others. There was a removable white screen at the back for film showings. The tiles in the entrance area had been replaced with a marble floor leading to a set of three steps. The cross-shaped transept had become the auditorium, with seats arranged in a horseshoe and little red and gold stucco decorations on the pillars. All the doors were self-closing. The ceiling was covered in dried teak and the discreet and respectful soundproofing diminished vocal sounds only to make them go further. Temístocles explained with false modesty that he had given the whole theatre an 'intimate feel', stage and auditorium both sharing a Franciscan sobriety.

'Of course it's closer to art than architecture,' he concluded.

The delegation inspected every detail. The leader of the group complimented Temístocles and, remembering the burglars, made a few comments about vandalism. He claimed to be a lover of buildings, a proponent of progress, a man of ideals, and declared he would have thrown himself into the study of the art of buildings if politics, duty, affairs of state, that whole other architecture had not, alas, taken him along a different path. They broached the subject of the grand opening and, without naming a date, Temístocles assured them that the work would be finished on time.

The only person unable to celebrate this new page in the nation's history was Don Octavio. Hidden away in silent, devoted solitude, he was busily screwing together upturned maplechairs. Sitting cross-legged like a hermit in his shack, with a long beard and hair down to his shoulders, he was writing history in his own way. His body was covered in marks, formed one by one like the letters of a story. Writing was expressed in his heart by varnish and acid, paint and wood, gold and lead. He sanded, scrubbed, carved out space, created a new grammar. A watering can made his rivers, a golden frame his mountains. He recorded light with an eyeglass and loupe.

Yet his arm became stiff. When he tried to stretch it out, it no longer extended fully. The handkerchief tied around it began to come loose, and he gently undid it.

One by one, shreds of cloth fell in ribbons onto the floor, landing among the sawdust and straw from chair seats. No blood, no scars, no scab. The fabric was clean and there was no sign of injury to his arm. But when he held it up to the light, Octavio saw that a layer of grey bark both bound and unbound its own skin to his.

The wood looked like alder, very dry, not resinous. A dense, almost brown cluster of thick, finely grooved layers that became more supple at the elbow to allow it to bend. The wrist was tattooed with knots. The arm sounded hollow when Octavio knocked on it, so he leant it on the table, picked up a handsaw and cut into his palm. At his core was solid wood. Gone were the bones, muscles and veins: autumn lay inside him.

Not wishing to be seen, he no longer left the side room. He came alive at night, fasting during the day and roaming the empty theatre during the evening, nibbling discarded crusts of bread. Outside, workdays were easy now, spent drinking beer and playing dominoes; idleness reigned. Soon the labourers were replaced by skilled workers, and there were no more men in blue overalls. Standing in the shadows, Octavio heard the directors' discussions in their offices, the swish of the actresses' costumes, the footsteps of guards on patrol. The fabric of the building was changing around him, too.

Within two days, the wood had gone beyond the elbow and had almost reached the shoulder. Its surface was so smooth that he used a chamois cloth soaked with linseed oil to polish himself. He dusted his four fingers with a brush and groomed himself with white vinegar. He found candle wax too gritty and used soapy water instead. Rather than sand himself, he buffed himself with a toothbrush. There he was, bent over, his ablutions now akin to the work of an antiquarian, as if cleaning a relic. After a week, there was ivy creeping from his feet to his knees and he realised he was growing like a tree that sprouts on a hill or in the middle of a building site, fading in the same spot where it took root.

Temístocles Jerez had agreed to let him stay at the theatre until the day after the official opening.

'After that, you'll need to find somewhere else,' he had told him amicably. 'You can't sleep here any more.'

Octavio had hidden, still, in the darkness. He smelt the musty odour he now gave off. His sweat, his breath, everything was covered in dust. Like the effigy of a forgotten world, all that was left of him was a smell of plaster and light.

*

The sky cleared on the morning of the opening day, but by the afternoon it had clouded over again.

Watching through the little window at ground level in the side room, Octavio saw the procession arrive with ministers, heads of institutions and the official press at the front. Next came, in order of importance, general secretaries, a few public figures and, in the middle of this phalanx, the mayor, dressed in red with a military helmet on his head. And finally, bringing up the rear, were the plodding ranks of the masses, the inhabitants of San Pablo del Limón.

Having taken his place in the dress circle, the minister began heaping compliments upon the architect. He wished to know the subject of the play. Someone referred to it as a bedroom farce, to much laughter.

They talked of the age of the governor Don Manuel González Torres de Navarro and the first theatres in the city, when Caracas was represented with a book in her hand and a lion at her feet. The mayor told a story about Baron von Humboldt, who had come to study satellites and discovered stars in Venezuelan melodramas that he had failed to spot in the sky. Someone else brought up the 1812 earthquake. They all agreed that theatre was the only thing that could survive natural disaster and colonisation.

When the curtain went up, everyone fell silent.

The play began in the port of La Guaira, on 20 August 1908, when a ship from Trinidad dropped anchor off the Venezuelan coast, unaware that it was offloading a plague which would trouble the country for half a century.

Beneath the roof of the new theatre, the company acted out a ferocious epidemic. With great commotion, a gang of sailors appeared on stage, and twisted columns and side panels were mechanically manoeuvred into place. Women in crinolines surrounded men in suits. The whole auditorium was filled with the smell of orchids. Beneath a row of streamers attached to the balconies, four musicians played a tragic Joropo. When the cardboard lemon tree arrived on stage, it was met with applause.

Temístocles went to find Octavio in the side room. Finding it empty, he searched the whole theatre, looking down all the corridors and everywhere backstage. The costume designer told him he was by the box office. At the box office, they said they had seen him in the wings. But as he made his way behind the stage, Temístocles saw in the footlights four men lifting the statue of the Nazarene of St Paul, sparkling with its legends.

The statue was carried in a procession across the stage, right to the edge of the orchestra pit. At that moment, the orchids, the songs, the lemon tree, everything the tired century had forgotten seemed to come back to life. The people were not celebrating a victory or anointing a king. Today, they were celebrating the birth of a city, a story not found in any book but built on tradition, whose invisible actors are worthy of honour.

Temístocles Jerez gave up his search. Perhaps he alone understood that beneath the wood of the statue, Octavio's heart continued to beat.